Copyright 2015 by Michelle St. James aka Michelle Zink

Cover design by Isabel Robalo

ISBN 978-0-9966056-6-3

D0913858

# 1

Angel Rossi opened her eyes all at once, fighting disorientation in the moment before she remembered where she was; the sofa in her office —formerly her father's office.

It wasn't unusual for her to take a nap in the middle of the night and then work until morning when she would run home for a shower and change of clothes. In the four months since she'd taken over her father's businesses — and the Syndicate's Boston territory — she'd spent almost every waking hour at Rossi Development.

She stretched and checked her phone. Two am, which meant she'd been dozing for almost two hours. She would need to work through the night to finish auditing the financials on the subsidiary that looked to be an off-the-books payroll service for the crooked cops who had worked for her father.

She wondered if Luca was still in the office next door. He'd been her almost constant companion since Nico's death, but she would have to send him back soon. Allow him to run New York properly, the way Nico had intended when he'd appointed Luca Underboss before his death.

*Nico...*

She shouldn't have worried that she would forget him. She could see his face as clearly as if she'd seen him yesterday, could still feel his hands on her naked body, his breath against her hair when he pulled her close in the middle of the night. He was as real as ever, and sometimes the permanence of his absence hit her out of the blue, the worst kind of surprise. She would double over then, heaving, gasping for air, sure the blood was turning to sludge in her veins, that her heart was slowly coming to a stop without him.

She was always surprised when she woke up the next morning. She forced herself to put one foot in front of the other even when it seemed impossible. It was what Nico would want, and she focused with obsessive single-mindedness on remaking her father's empire — and plotting revenge against the people who had supported Dante in his bid to oust Nico.

Raneiro had come to visit shortly after she'd removed Frank Morra. The head of the Syndicate had been impassive as he'd quizzed her about her plans for the Boston territory. She wasn't fooled. Possession was nine-tenths of the law, and right now, she was in possession of Boston. But she knew he had concerns. Her father hadn't intended for her to take over when he died, hadn't even bothered to tell Angel about his business with the Syndicate. She knew Raneiro thought she was in over her head.

It might have been true in the beginning, when she'd been driven more by fury than ambition. But her anger had fueled a sustained determination to dismantle the machine that had killed Nico and ruined her chances of having a normal life. That had traumatized David to the point that he could hardly leave the brownstone even now, months after Dante kidnapped him and cut off two of his fingers in an effort to gain control of the New York territory.

Dante had been the head of the snake, but he hadn't been alone. Men from other families had joined him in an effort to kill Nico's twenty-first century business model for the Syndicate — a model that was seen as too soft by men accustomed to the brutality of old world organized crime. They had all worked with Dante in one capacity or another. Offered him help, support, resources. She had made it her mission to destroy every one of them.

She started by learning the books at Rossi Development inside and out. Learning where the money was hidden, how it was laundered. Learning which cops were on the payroll, which men had aided her father in the murder of Nico's parents. Now she knew who was involved in the most despicable of the Syndicate's income streams — child pornography, human trafficking, bad loans to those already down on their luck, identity theft of innocent people.

And she was slowly picking at the threads that would unravel it all.

She sat up as something rustled nearby. Was it outside the office? The janitors usually didn't come until later, and everyone else was gone except Luca. He rarely left her alone, and when he did go back to the apartment he was renting downtown, he made sure Marco or Elia had eyes on her. It had been disconcerting at first, but she'd gotten used to it. After what happened in Los Angeles, she didn't trust anyone but them, and she needed to stay alive long enough to finish the job she'd started and make sure David was back on his feet.

She heard the sound again, then saw something shift out of the corner of her eye. She stood, heart pounding, and reached for the gun she'd set on the coffee table before she'd gone to sleep. She'd rejected David's suggestion that she might have PTSD, too. That she could benefit from counseling. She'd gone to the shooting range instead, hired an instructor, practiced until she had a ninety percent kill ratio at seventy-five feet.

She scanned the office, her eyes coming to rest on a shadowy figure leaning against the wall across from her.

She raised the gun, thumbed off the safety. "I suggest you identify yourself," she said. "Unless you'd like your DNA to do it for you."

The figure stepped forward, arms raised in surrender, hands empty. But that was all easy to register, easier than the face that slowly came into view in the faint light spilling from the lamp on the desk.

She shook her head. "No. It... It can't be."

He stepped closer, and she was assaulted by the smell of him, the scent of leather and soap and something else now. Pine?

He gently took the gun from her hand and set it back on the coffee table. Then he met her gaze, and she knew it was true. His face was thinner, but it was him, the amber eyes piercing hers in the darkness, the set of his shoulders as uncompromising as ever under his white T-shirt and a familiar leather jacket.

He touched his knuckles to her face, ran them gently down her cheek, his eyes locked on hers. She couldn't breathe, didn't dare move. She registered with detachment that her face was wet, tears streaming from her eyes.

"I'm sorry, Angel," he said.

She lifted a hand and cracked it hard across his face.

# 2

Nico stared after her, listened to the sound of her heels clicking on the marble floor of the lobby before she disappeared into the elevator. When she was gone, he paced to the window overlooking downtown Boston. It was pretty, but it wasn't New York. He missed it. Missed the chaos and noise, the honking and swearing, the history that was baked and frozen into the concrete and stone.

He hadn't been back since before he and Angel left for Miami just before summer. Then there was the frantic trip to LA to save David, the chaos of his rescue, the aftermath that Nico had been forced to watch from afar.

He slipped a hand into the pocket of his jeans, touched the rosary beads he sometimes carried there. He still wasn't sure he believed in god, but the beads had brought him comfort during the long months when he'd been alone. It was some combination of the repetition as he slid them through his fingers, the memories they brought of childhood when everything had seemed so simple.

Angel didn't understand. He couldn't blame her. Faking his death had been a last resort. The only way he felt sure she would be safe — and the only way he stood a chance of figuring out what was really going on in the Syndicate.

He'd known as soon as they got to LA that the conspiracy against him went deeper than Dante and a handful of traitors from various families. The effort to sabotage the Vitale family had required too much manpower, too many resources, to be attributed to Dante alone. Something bigger was happening behind the scenes, and Nico had no doubt that once they rescued David, he would be next on the list.

And whoever came for him wouldn't be satisfied with a couple of fingers.

He didn't care about himself. If he'd been alone, he would have surrounded himself by the men he trusted, brushed up on his Eskrima and tactical training, taken his chances.

But he couldn't do that with Angel. Wouldn't.

He didn't know if she intended to stay with him after her brother was rescued, but it didn't matter. Whoever was after him knew that she was his weakness, and that meant she was a target as long as he was alive.

He and Luca had started formulating the plan in the days they spent at Locke's beach house before David's rescue. Luca hadn't liked it. Hell, Nico wasn't exactly thrilled either. But it had seemed the only way to put meaningful distance between him and Angel. To buy him time to do some real investigation into what was going on. It hadn't been a guarantee of her safety, and he'd made damn sure Luca had someone on her 24/7 ever since, but Nico had bet on the fact that with him out of the picture, his enemies would be satisfied with keeping an eye on Angel, at least for awhile.

He'd been right, but now their time was up. Nico would let her calm down, and then he'd explain. She'd understand. She'd have to.

He turned to face the luxurious office where Angel spent most of her time. It wasn't the first time he'd been there since she took over Rossi Development and the Boston family. Luca kept him informed about Angel's movements, and Nico had gotten good at watching her in the post-midnight hours when she slept on the sofa in her father's old office. He'd just needed to see her up close. To see the way pieces of her hair fell out of the bun at the back of her head, the childlike way she folded her legs under her while she slept. She looked so different then. Different from the way she looked marching into the office in the mornings, her face an expressionless mask.

He almost hadn't recognized her the first time he'd dared to watch from the sidewalk as she entered the building. She'd looked so focused, so emotionless, so devoid of the vulnerability that made him want to end anyone who so much as hurt her feelings.

But when she slept he could see her the way she had been in his bed. Then he remembered the feel of her porcelain skin under his palm, her body moving under his as she welcomed him into her moist heat, her passionate cries as she came apart in his hands.

She belonged to him. Being without her had felt like missing a piece of himself. It was the worst kind of phantom limb, a dull ache in his chest that was a constant reminder of her absence. He'd spent the last four months skulking in the shadows, sleeping in dingy hotel rooms, eating shitty food while Luca ran New York under Raneiro's watchful eyes.

And he'd done it for her. To ensure that she was safe, that she stayed that way.

He would just have to make her see it. It didn't matter whether she forgave him. Not really. What mattered was letting her know the extent of the danger she was in. And eliminating that danger once and for all.

His phone vibrated in his pocket. He reached for it with one hand while heading for the door.

"What is it?"

He listened to the voice on the other end of the phone. Five seconds later he was running for the elevator.

# 3

Luca was leaning against the building, hands in the pockets of his leather jacket, when she stepped outside. She stopped in front of him, her heart racing so fast she thought it might beat out of her chest.

"You fucking asshole," she said, her voice low.

He opened his mouth to speak, but she was already moving past him, down the sidewalk toward the brownstone that had been in her family since she was born.

"I'm sorry," he called after her.

She heard his footsteps on the pavement, and a moment later he was walking next to her, his long legs easily keeping pace even though she was practically running to get away from him.

They walked together in tense silence for a couple of minutes, the city dark and quiet except for the street lights and an occasional car. Usually she liked walking home in the dark, even if Luca or one of the other men was always on her heels. But now she was almost shaking, her mind and body overwhelmed with Nico's sudden reappearance.

"How could you?" she finally said without looking at Luca.

"I had no choice."

"Bullshit," she said as they turned the corner. "You let me think he was dead. You…" She inhaled a deep, shuddering breath, dimly aware that her anger was the only thing keeping darker emotions at bay. "You let me go to his funeral. Let me think I was burying him."

She had a flash of the coffin, the smell of the grass when she'd gone to the cemetery that night, the hole that opened up inside her when she thought she was leaving Nico's body there.

"I know," he said. "But this is bigger than the two of you."

"Sounds like a cop out," she said.

"It's not. You're just going to have to trust me on that."

"Well, I don't." She practically spat the words as she crossed her arms in front of her. "Not anymore."

He didn't say anything, but she felt him tense next to her. They'd become close in Nico's absence. Or she thought they had anyway. Luca had been the one constant in her life, and her most powerful connection to Nico. She couldn't even fathom the extent of his deceit. All the times she'd been sad and lonely. All the times she missed Nico so much she didn't think the blood would keep flowing through her veins. Luca had known Nico was alive and said nothing.

They continued down Commonwealth until they came to the brownstone. In the spring, cherry blossoms colored the trees outside pink. Now everything was pale and green, on the verge of the riot of color that would signify fall.

She stopped at the steps leading up to the front door and turned to face him. "Does Marco know?" she asked. "Elia?"

He shook his head, and she saw the regret in his eyes. "I'm the only one."

She thought about that, about Nico in hiding for four months with no one but Luca to know he was alive. But no. She couldn't start feeling sorry for him. He had done this. He and Luca. And they had put her through hell.

"Go home, Luca," she said.

"Can't do it." His blue eyes flashed under the shock of dark hair. "Boss's orders."

The words called forth a fresh wave of indignity.

"I don't think you understand." She spoke slowly, evenly. She had become one of them, the measure of her fury evident in the level of calm forced into her voice. "*I* am the boss. Now go home."

She headed for the house, but when she got to the front door, she looked back to find him leaning against the iron fence next door. Of course, he wouldn't leave. It pissed her off, but there was nothing she could do about it. She'd learned not to bring attention to herself, to Rossi Development, to any of their business dealings or associates. Being part of the Syndicate meant being subject to rules and limitations that made even the most straightforward of situations seem complicated.

Fine. Let him stand out there all night then.

She opened the door and locked it behind her, then stood listening in the entry. The house was quiet. David was probably upstairs in his room, watching Netflix or sleeping off the anti-depressants prescribed to him by the psychiatrist he'd been seeing since he got out of the hospital. She hung her coat near the door and made her way up the stairs.

David's medication made her nervous, especially since she was at the office so much of the time. She made sure to check on him several times a day, but she still lived in fear that he would accidentally take too many of the pills — or that maybe it wouldn't be an accident at all. He'd been kidnapped and tortured. Had lost two of his fingers, been afraid for his life before he was rescued in the hail of bullets that had finally killed Dante Santoro. David wasn't himself, might never be himself again because of her.

She shook the thought from her mind as she reached the second floor landing. She couldn't look back. She'd done what seemed right at the time: helping Nico, trying to figure out who was targeting him. She couldn't have known Dante would come after David. She couldn't have known any of it would happen like it did; that she would kill the man standing between her and Nico, that she would require two hours of emergency surgery to remove the bullet he'd fired into her stomach on his way down. It had been traumatic for all of them, but most of all for David who had gone from being a college student grieving his father's death to being held hostage by one of the Syndicate's most brutal men.

She stopped at the closed door of his room and listened for a few seconds before rapping softly on the carved wood. No answer. She tried again, then eased open the door.

The room was dark, the heavy curtains pulled shut like always. It didn't matter if it was nine in the morning or six at night, David's room was always cloaked in darkness, as if the thick velvet draperies could keep his fear at bay.

He was laying on his back, light brown hair flopping onto his forehead, lanky limbs splayed out across the mattress. He'd always slept that way. When they were little and could convince their mother to let them sleep in the same bed, Angel never lasted long before retreating to her own room. David had been a bed hog even then.

His left hand was still wrapped in a bandage, even though it had mostly healed. She thought it was because he didn't want to look at his disfigured hand, didn't want to admit it was permanent, and she felt ashamed at her relief that the bandage meant she didn't have to admit it either.

"David," she said softly, lowering herself onto the mattress next to him. She touched his hair, said his name again.

He stirred, and a split second later his eyes flew open and he sat up, terror playing across his features in the dim light making its way into the room from the sconces in the hallway.

She put a hand on his shoulder. "It's okay," she said. "It's just me."

He lay back down, his body slowly relaxing. "What time is it?"

"It's the middle of the night." She felt guilty as she said it. Why did she wake him up? Was she scared he'd OD on his medication? Or was she just looking for company? "I'm sorry."

"It's okay," he said. "Is everything all right?"

She fought the urge to laugh hysterically. "It's fine," she said softly. "I was just checking on you. Go back to sleep."

He nodded and rolled over. "Love you, Ange."

She ruffled his hair. "Love you, too, loser."

He snorted into his pillow as she eased from the room.

She closed his door and headed back downstairs. It was nearly four am, but she wasn't ready for sleep, and she continued toward the kitchen at the back of the house.

She still wasn't used to being back in Boston. Filled with antiques and art chosen by her father's decorator, the house felt stiff in a way Nico's family home in the Hudson Valley hadn't. But she hadn't had time to redecorate, hadn't had energy for anything except taking care of David and plotting revenge against the men who had betrayed Nico. She felt a sudden longing for her little apartment upstate; the tiny bedroom, the living room with the threadbare thrift store couch. It hadn't been much, but it had been hers, and it had been bought and paid for honestly. She had already packed up her father's penthouse apartment. She would need to do something about the brownstone eventually, too.

She pulled a bottle of wine from the fridge, and poured a healthy sized glass. Her hands shook as she brought it to her mouth, and she took a long swallow before setting it back on the counter. Her nerves smoothed out just in time for reality to hit her.

Nico was alive.

She closed her eyes against the memories. Nico's perfect body moving over her, his breath in her ear, his strong hands spreading her thighs.

A sob escaped her mouth, and she bent over at the waist, muffling her cries against her hand. Waves of emotion crashed over her; anger and relief and bitterness all mixed together in a hurricane that threatened to undo the facade of control she'd constructed over the past four months. It went on and on, the pain of losing him wracking her body while her mind tried to reconcile it with the fact that he had been alive all this time.

*Alive, alive, alive…*

She was suddenly overwhelmed with the need to see him. What had she been thinking when she'd walked away? She needed him in front of her, needed to know it was real. Then she would deal with the why of it all.

She straightened, wiping her mouth with the back of her hand and taking a deep cleansing breath. She was reaching for her cell phone when glass exploded behind her head.

# 4

She hit the floor almost without thinking, instinctively covering her head to shield her face from the falling glass. More of it erupted from a second window in the kitchen, and then she understood; someone was shooting at her.

She crawled toward a drawer next to the fridge as another volley of gunfire erupted, wood splintering from the cabinets overhead. When she got to the drawer, she slid it open from the floor and reached into the back where she kept a twenty-two caliber revolver. She'd learned to appreciate the sense of protection the gun offered her. Luca or one of the other guys was almost always in close proximity, but she wasn't about to leave their safety up to someone else. Not after all they'd been through.

Luca… Was he still out front? Had he heard the explosion of gunfire from the back of the house? Had someone taken him out on their way to the back yard. She fought panic at the thought that something might have happened to him, forced herself to push it aside. Leaning against the fridge, she checked the gun to make sure it was still loaded, then took a deep breath while she assessed the situation.

So far only one gunman, but that didn't mean there weren't more of them outside. She thought of David upstairs in bed. Was he drugged enough that he'd stay asleep? Panic hit her full force as she imagined him stumbling down the stairs to investigate the noise. He would be an easy target, completely unable to protect himself.

"Please stay put, David," she muttered under her breath, crawling to the edge of the cabinets that made up the kitchen island. They were protecting her from the now empty window casings, but they also blocked her view.

She dared a glance around the island and was met with a hail of splintering wood from above. So someone had a good view of her position then. Great. She was a sitting duck, trapped in the kitchen, unable to get to David and escape the house without risking another round of gunfire. The lights were on, but it was dark outside, which meant she couldn't see a thing beyond the windows while whoever was shooting at her could see everything. She'd basically given them a spotlight. They had her on the defensive, and that was never a position of power.

She was leaning forward again, preparing to crawl for the stairs, get to David where she stood a better chance of protecting him — or at least keeping him from walking into a firestorm — when the lights went out. A split second later, someone grabbed her from behind. The urge to scream was reflexive, but a hand was clamped over her mouth before she got the chance.

"Shhhh…" a familiar voice said in her ear. "It's me."

*Nico…*

She twisted a little to look at him, and he removed his hand from her mouth.

"What are you doing here?" she hissed.

"I came to tell you someone was trying to kill me — and maybe you — but I think it's a little late for that," he said drily. "And you're welcome."

"You're welcome? You haven't done anything yet," she said.

"I just got here." He pushed her behind him. Something shimmered in the faint light of the now darkened kitchen, and she saw that he had a gun, too. "I'll cover you while you get David."

"Then what?"

"Then you stay put until I come for you," he said. "Is there a way out from upstairs?"

"There's an old staircase at the back. A servant's staircase, I think."

"Where does it lead?" he asked.

She thought about the brownstone. "Here in the kitchen, to that door." She tipped her head toward a closed door. "And also… to the cellar, I think."

"Is there an exit in the cellar?" he asked.

"I have no idea."

He nodded. "We'll figure it out. Just make a run for it when I start shooting, and stay put with David until I come for you."

She wasn't crazy about leaving Nico to fight her battle while she hid upstairs, but keeping David safe was her number one priority.

"Okay," she said, kicking off her heels.

"On my count," he said. "Three, two, one…"

He peered around the counter and started firing in the direction of the windows. She scurried on all fours to the protection of the hallway, the gun still in her hand. She was hurrying up the stairs when she heard gunfire explode outside the foyer. She thought someone might be trying to get in through the front door, but then she heard answering shots from another location beyond it and realized there were multiple people shooting at the front of the house. How long would it take the police to get here? Or had they been paid for a delay by whoever orchestrated the attack?

She couldn't rule it out. Anything was possible with the Syndicate.

She hit the second floor landing at a run and burst into David's room. He was sitting on the bed, backed up against the headboard, his face frozen in cold terror.

"It's okay." She rushed into the room, never so grateful for David's instance on keeping the drapes drawn. "We're going to get out of here."

He stared straight ahead, his eyes glazed over, as she took hold of his arm.

"Come on. We have to go. Get your shoes." He didn't move, and she leaned down so she could look him in the eyes. "Look at me, David. Now."

His eyes seemed to clear, and he cut his gaze to hers.

"It's going to be okay, but we have to get out of here. All right?"

His nod was reluctant, but at least he was responding.

"Where are your shoes?" she asked him.

"Closet," he croaked, his eyes widening as another round of gunfire burst from the first floor of the house.

She crossed the room and opened his closet door, then removed a pair of sneakers. She set them on the floor and pulled his legs around so his feet were next to the shoes.

"Put those on," she said. "And hurry."

He started moving — too slow for her liking, but at least he was moving — and she crossed to the window, daring a peek around the curtains. Everything was dark, still no sign of the police. Shots burst from the front of the house below David's window, and for a split second she caught a flash of someone's face in the glow of the firing gun. It was a man, but the light didn't last long enough for her to get a good look at him.

"Ange?" She turned toward the sound of David's voice. "I put on my shoes."

She nodded and walked over to him. "Good."

Glancing down at his clothes, she saw that he was in a pair of old pajama pants and a T-shirt. She went to his dresser and pulled out some jeans and T-shirts, then shoved them into a backpack from David's closet.

Where was Nico? How long was she supposed to wait?

She was debating the merit of trying to get David out of the house on her own when Nico burst through the door. His face was calm, his eyes intense, and she felt an immediately lightening of her fear. It was the kind of safety she only ever felt with him.

"Let's go," he said calmly.

She turned to her brother and handed him the backpack. "Come on."

He was paralyzed again, his body frozen as he looked at Nico, and she realized he had no idea Nico was still alive. It must have been like literally seeing a ghost.

"It's okay. I'll explain later. Nico's going to get us out of here." Another volley of gunfire exploded below the house, and she thought she heard the front door splinter. She tugged on David's arm. "Come *on,* David."

He let her pull him up from the bed and they joined Nico at the door. He stuck his head out into the hall, then turned back to them.

"Stay close." He moved out of the room.

# 5

Nico led the way down the narrow back staircase with one thought in his mind: get Angel and her brother out alive. Thank god she lived only a few minutes from the offices of Rossi Development. He'd hit the street at a dead run after receiving Luca's call saying two men were moving into position outside the brownstone. He'd arrived just as the gunman at the back of the house fired on Angel.

He came to a stop at the landing behind the kitchen and turned to Angel and David, then put a finger to his lips, listening for clues about what was going on outside. They were ill-prepared; too few men, no headsets, no plan for escape. He heard the sound of gunfire, but it sounded farther away. At the front of the house? Fuck. He couldn't be sure from the muffled confines of the staircase, but he couldn't afford to cower. He needed to move Angel and her brother out of the house, get them to safety before things got worse.

"As long as the coast is clear, we're going to exit through the doors in the kitchen. Stay close, stay low, and do whatever I say." He cut a glance at David, who was pale and trembling. "Are you okay?"

He didn't answer, and Angel took his arm. "He'll be okay," she said. "Just get us out of here."

Nico eased open the door and looked into the dark kitchen. It was quiet, but that didn't mean someone wasn't watching. He slipped out of the staircase, waved Angel and David forward behind him, and entered the kitchen at a crouch, his gun trained on the shattered windows.

Nothing.

Had he hit the man who had been firing at Angel from the backyard? Or had the man gone to the front to assist whoever was firing from there?

No way for Nico to know until he exposed himself. And Angel.

He moved toward the set of doors leading to the backyard. They were almost there when glass exploded from inside the mullions. Fire ripped through his left arm as he shoved Angel and David back against the wall and returned fire. He couldn't see shit, but he fired in the direction of the shots as he covered Angel and her brother.

A minute later, the shooting stopped. Had the gunman gone down, hit by one of Nico's bullets? Or was he waiting for them to leave the house?

He took a deep breath and eased toward the door with Angel and David on his heels. He didn't bother opening it, just cleared the little bit of remaining glass with his hand and stepped through the ruined frame, trying to keep Angel and David behind him.

Nothing.

He glanced back. "Come on."

He hurried down the terrace steps and stepped onto a crushed gravel pathway that led to the front of the house. He'd used it to enter the living room window from the side of the house while Angel had been under fire in the kitchen. He led them that way and almost tripped over a prone figure sprawled half in the bushes and half in the path.

Blood was oozing from a wound in the man's chest and trickling out of the corner of his mouth. His eyes were closed, but he was alive, a low groan coming from his mouth. Nico had never seen the man before. He'd undoubtedly been sent by someone more powerful. But he had tried to kill Angel. Had made her cower and fear for her life. For the life of her brother. And that meant he wouldn't be allowed to leave alive.

Nico raised his weapon and fired into the man's forehead. He went still, and Nico waved Angel and David forward.

"Come on."

Nico half-expected to hear gunfire as they reached the front of the house, but it was quiet when they rounded the corner.

"You're clear," a voice said to his left.

"Luca!" There was obvious relief in Angel's voice. Nico wondered if this meant she would forgive him for the secret Nico had forced his friend to keep. He hoped so.

"You didn't think I'd really leave you alone, did you?" Luca asked.

Nico looked him over. He was disheveled but none the worse for wear.

"Where'd the other one go?" Nico asked.

"Took off," Luca said. "What about the one in back?"

"Dead," Nico said.

In the distance, the sound of sirens erupted into the night.

"Time's up," Luca said. He handed Nico a set of keys. "Car's around the block. You need to get out of here."

Nico nodded. "Thanks."

He didn't ask about Luca. He didn't need to. After so many years working together, the words were unspoken but understood; Nico would get Angel and her brother to safety. Luca could take care of himself. They would connect when they could through channels that had been set up long ago for just this kind of situation.

Luca clapped his shoulder. "It's nothing. Keep in touch."

He walked away, disappearing into the night a few seconds later.

Nico turned to Angel and David. "Let's go."

They hurried around the corner where a black Escalade was waiting. They got in the car and were making a U-turn as the first squad car crossed the intersection behind them. Nico kept his speed down, careful not to draw attention as they put distance between themselves and the brownstone. He glanced over at Angel, drinking her in from the glow of streetlights on the other side of the glass. She was as lovely as he remembered, as lovely as she'd looked all the times he'd watched her in secret. She was a bit thinner, her cheekbones more pronounced, but she was still his Angel, her hair the color of sunlight in fall, her eyes as green as the deepest waters of the Atlantic.

He was surprised to find that she didn't look shaken. In fact, her face was so serene, he didn't notice the gun in her hand right away. She held it against her thigh as easily as if it were a set of keys. He reached for it, prying it from her fingers and setting it inside the console. Then he took her hand and squeezed.

"Everything's going to be okay," he said.

He headed for the highway and the one place they would be safe.

# 6

She knew right away where they were going. The few times she'd
been able to get away from Rossi Development and the Syndicate,
she'd gone to Nico's island in Maine. It was the place she felt closest
to him, and she'd spent the time walking the beaches with David,
telling him all the good things about Nico, not wanting her brother to
remember the man she loved as a thug who had killed their father,
destroyed their lives.

She told him the whole truth instead: that their father had
murdered Nico's parents and Nico had sought revenge by
kidnapping her. That he'd saved her life when their father had held a
gun to her head. That he'd saved David's life in Los Angeles and
made it possible for them to be free of Dante by killing him.

She didn't reinvent Nico. She didn't need to. He had shown
her how enigmatic people could be. The beauty of him was in his
mystery, and she didn't want to do him the disservice of
oversimplifying him to David. To anyone.

She turned around in the front seat to look at her brother as
they made the turnoff for Bass Harbor, Maine. He was pale and
sickly looking, the bandage on his hand limp and dirty. Guilt wound
its way through her stomach. She'd been too busy with the
Syndicate's business — too focused on those responsible for Nico's

death — to properly look after David. He'd been stuck in the brownstone, afraid and alone, and while she'd taken him to therapy, had tried to come home for the occasional meal, she hadn't spent enough time coaxing him out of his shell. She wondered what kind of damage the shootout at the brownstone had done to him, how far back it would set the healing process.

"You okay?" she asked him as they got out of the car in the parking lot above the harbor.

He nodded, but she could see the fine sheen of sweat on his upper lip, and his eyes were wide and startled.

She took his arm. "It's all right," she told him. "We'll be safe now."

It was almost noon, but the wind was cold, and she was glad they'd found a mini-mart on the road where she could buy a cheap pair of sweats and tennis shoes. She zipped up the sweatshirt over her blouse and stayed close to David as they made their way down to the waterfront.

Ed, the wizened man who ferried them back and forth to the island, was waiting when they got to the dock. They piled into the boat, and Angel sat next to David, holding his hand as they sped across the water. It had been almost exactly a year since she'd made the trip for the first time with Nico. The bite of the wind and churning of the water was familiar, but everything else was different.

Nico had changed her. Or maybe he'd just shown her who she'd been all along.

She was still angry for what he'd done, but knowing him like she did, she had to believe there was a reason. It's a conclusion she would have reached in Boston if she'd had the time. Now she reveled in the site of him, standing tall and strong at the front of the boat.

He was a little leaner than he'd been the last time she'd seen him, but it did nothing to diminish the raw power of his physicality. His thighs strained against the fabric of his jeans, his leather jacket doing nothing to hide the significant breadth of his shoulders. His chiseled pecs were visible under the thin fabric of his white T-shirt, and she had a sudden memory; running her tongue from his chest to his throat, his body hard and insistent under her as she rode him, his hands wrapped in the hair at the back of her head, searing her with his gaze while he thrust up into her.

He was alive.

The truth of it almost took her breath away, and she squeezed David's hand to keep her own from shaking.

The island rose up out of the water like an emerald mirage. Ed slowed down, then coasted the last few feet to the small dock. Angel helped David out of the boat while Nico spoke quietly to Ed. Then Ed was heading back toward open water.

Nico picked up David's backpack and they headed for the woods surrounding the private residence that was Nico's refuge.

They arrived at the house twenty minutes later. Nico disabled the alarm, and they stepped into the stone entry, the Atlantic beckoning from behind the wall of glass in the living room. David seemed rooted to the ground, and Angel realized he hadn't spoken since they left Boston.

"It's okay," she said gently, leading him to the stairs. "Go upstairs. Take a shower, get some sleep. We'll talk later."

He followed her instructions like a child, his movements slow and deliberate as he made his way up the stairs. She waited until she heard the click of his bedroom door to continue into the living room. David always slept in the room Nico had given Angel the first time he'd brought her here, before she'd accepted the inevitability of her attraction to him.

She was under no such delusion now. She would have it out with Nico. Find out why he'd done what he'd done. Rail at him for putting her through it. Then he would lead her to the master suite, take off her clothes, remind her that she was still his.

That she always had been. That she always would be.

She stood watching him as he loaded the fireplace with wood and old newspaper. He'd taken off his jacket, and the muscle and tendons in his back flexed as he placed everything in the grate. He'd only been grazed by the bullet that hit him at the brownstone, and they had cleaned and wrapped the wound in the bathroom of the mini-mart where they'd stopped for gas. Now she was afraid to take her eyes off him. Afraid he would disappear into thin air. Had he been here during the last four months? Had he stood on the beach under the house only hours after she and David left? Had he missed her as much as she'd missed him?

He lit a match, held it to the newspaper, then stepped back as it spread to the kindling, and finally, the bigger pieces of wood.

She crossed the room, stood next to him and watched the firelight play across his face. "Tell me."

He hesitated, then turned to look at her. He took her face in his hands, staring at her with something hungry and desperate in the moment before he lowered his lips to hers. She melted against him, forcing her mind to stay clear while he claimed her mouth with a mixture of tenderness and barely controlled desire. She was relieved when he didn't lead her straight to bed. She needed to hear what he had to say — to know that everything she'd been through had been for a good reason — and she wouldn't be able to think straight once he really started touching her.

He rubbed his thumb along her swollen lower lip, and she clenched her thighs together to stop the pulse of her body calling for him.

He turned away and headed for the liquor-topped cabinet. "Drink?"

"Please," she said.

He poured whiskey into two glasses, crossed the room, and handed her one of them. "You might want to sit down."

# 7

She wanted to snap at him. To tell him she wasn't the scared girl he'd once known. But she suddenly felt anything but strong, her guard slowly slipping in the presence of his strength.

She sat at one end of the couch and was glad when he took the other end. She didn't need the distraction. Didn't want to smell him, to feel the magnetic pull of her body to his.

He downed the drink in one swallow and ran one hand through his dark hair. "I knew Los Angeles wouldn't be the end of it," he finally said.

"What do you mean?" she asked.

He stared into the fire, now devouring the wood he'd stacked inside the grate. "Dante was just an instrument."

"We already knew he wasn't acting alone," Angel said. At least ten men had defected from the Vitale family — and some from other families as well — in the months before Dante kidnapped David in an effort to take over the Syndicate's New York territory.

"We knew there were followers, disciples of Dante who wanted to see the business return to its traditions," Nico clarified. "We didn't know someone else was orchestrating the movement."

"Someone above Dante?" Angel asked.

Nico nodded. "After we got David out alive, I needed to be invisible for awhile to figure out what was really going on."

"And did you?" she asked.

"I'm not sure."

"Then why come back?" The question sounded more bitter than she intended. Happy wasn't a strong enough word to describe how she felt now that she knew he was alive. But she'd gotten used to her grief, her bitterness. What was she supposed to do with all of that now?

He sighed. "I spent the last four months tracing the hierarchy above Dante, trying to figure out where the orders were coming from. Then Luca heard through the grapevine that a hit had been taken out on you."

She sat up straighter, the liquor turning sour in her stomach. "On me?"

He nodded. "And David."

"By who?"

He turned to look at her. "By the same person who wanted me dead back when we rescued David."

She shook her head, running through a list of names in her mind before skidding to a stop on one of them. "Raneiro?"

"The one and only," Nico said, his voice laced with ice.

"But…" She shook her head. "Why? I mean, I know he wasn't convinced I could handle Boston when we kicked out Frank, but I've followed every rule to the letter. I've handed over the correct percentage of our profits to the Syndicate. I've escalated up line when the situation has called for it."

"Except with your first round of… eliminations," he said.

"Frank deserved to be kicked to the curb," she said coldly. "And so did every single person who was kicked there with him."

"I'm not disputing that," he said. "I'm not even saying that's why Raneiro came after you."

"Then what?"

"Raneiro has no reason to believe you're any different than me. It was no secret we were involved, and no secret that you were coming at the business with a different perspective than the men who've run it for generations. My vision for a new Syndicate hasn't played out to his liking. He's done. "

"So he was going to… what?" she asked. "Kill David and I to make sure the Rossis were done with the Boston territory for good?"

"That's what it looks like," Nico said. "He already thought I was out of the picture. Eliminating you would allow him to reinstate the old world model without resistance."

"You came out of hiding for me," she murmured.

He turned sharply toward her. "I wasn't in hiding, Angel." His voice was steely. "You know me better than that."

She nodded. Nico Vitale was not a man who hid. From anything.

"I did what I did to protect you while I figured out who was really responsible for the upheaval in the Syndicate. I needed perspective. The kind of perspective that I could only gain by removing myself from the situation, by looking at it from afar. And I needed to know you were safe while I got it."

She put down her empty glass and walked to the doors overlooking the beach. They'd traveled through the night, entered Maine as the sun rose into the sky. It felt like a lifetime since she'd been sleeping on the sofa in her office. Since she had thought Nico was dead. Too much had happened in too short a time. Her gut was still catching up to her brain.

"How did you do it?" she asked.

"I was wearing kevlar, like all the men," he said softly. "I didn't want to be shot, but Luca and I had planned for the possibility as a way for me to get out of the picture with minimal risk. After that it was just a little money in the right hands."

"And you couldn't tell me?" she asked softly. "I…" She exhaled a shuddering breath. "I didn't know how to live without you."

She closed her eyes as his hands came to rest on her shoulders. "But you did live, Angel. And I had to make sure it stayed that way. If you'd known I was alive…" He took a deep breath. "We wouldn't have remained apart for long. We would have met in secret. We might even have gotten away with it for awhile. But eventually someone would have found out, and then you would have been a target again because of your connection to me."

"I was a target anyway," she said, looking at his reflection in the glass.

*And I had to live without you every day.*

"I know." She felt the hard press of his thighs behind her legs, his chest as immoveable as stone against her back. "And I'm going to kill the bastards responsible."

She should have been scared by the promise in his voice, but that Angel was gone forever. Now she could only feel relieved. He would fight to keep her and David safe, and she would fight with him.

She turned in his arms, lacing her hands behind his neck, pressing her body against him. "Take me to bed, Nico. I don't want to talk about them anymore."

# 8

She didn't have to ask him twice. He lifted her into his arms and headed for the stairs, relishing the feel of her in his arms, her hair soft against his chin. He'd imagined this moment for the last four months, and he kept his eyes on hers, afraid she would disappear like a dream.

He walked past David's room and continued to the master suite. He used his foot to close the door behind them, then deposited Angel on the floor next to the bed. She stood there while he opened the curtains and the doors leading to the balcony. He wanted to see her clearly while he took her, wanted to relearn every inch of her body.

When he returned, he saw that she was shaking, and he put a hand on either side of her face, lowered his lips to hers, swept her mouth tenderly with his tongue.

"It's okay," he said when he pulled back. "I'm here."

He held her gaze while he unbuttoned the blouse she'd been wearing since the day before. The red silk slid off her shoulders and onto the floor, and he slipped the fleece pants they'd bought on their way to Maine past the curve of her hips. Rage filled him as he lingered over the scar on her stomach. He wanted to kill the man who did it all over again, and he said a silent prayer of thanks that

Angel's bullet had done the job on her way down. He gently kissed the scar, then drew in a ragged breath at the sight of her.

She stood before him in nothing but a bra and panties, two scraps of scarlet lace standing between him and nirvana. She had been the object of every dream, every desire, during his exile. Now he didn't know where to start. His cock strained against his jeans, begging for the release that only she could give him. He wanted both to claim her quickly and to savor every moment. Wanted to rip off the panties and plunge into her, and wanted to lick every inch of her body, explore every secret place to make sure it still belonged to him.

As if reading his thoughts, she reached behind her and unhooked the bra, throwing it to the floor. She took his hands, placed them on her breasts, full and heavy, her nipples pale and pink and already hard.

"I'm here, too," she said, her voice hoarse with desire.

He groaned, burying one hand in the hair at the back of her head while the other snaked around her waist, pulling her tight against him. He tugged at her hair, just enough to give him better access to the pale expanse of her neck. She moaned, and he lowered his lips to the hollow of her throat and kissed his way up her neck as she breathed fast and heavy.

"Nico..."

His name on her lips was the best kind of aphrodisiac. His cock pulsed between his legs, and he heard her gasp as he ran his tongue along the tender spot behind her ear, then kissed his way to her mouth. He was riveted to it. Couldn't take his eyes off her swollen lips. Couldn't stop thinking about how it felt to kiss her while he drove into her, how it felt when her lips were wrapped around his shaft, taking him all the way to the back of her throat, owning him like he owned her.

He cupped her face with his hands, ran his thumb along the corner of her mouth, drawing out the moment before he would really taste her. And then his mouth was on hers, her lips opening for him, pulling him into her warmth while he stroked her tongue with his. He swept and parried, his mouth falling back into the rhythm of tasting her like no time had passed.

This was his Angel. She belonged to him no matter what.

She slipped a hand between them and undid the button on his jeans, closed her hand around his cock. He groaned, pulsing in her hand while she sank her teeth gently into his lower lip. He couldn't take it. She was going to make him come before they even got started, and there was no way that's how this was going down.

He pushed her back on the bed and got rid of her panties with one quick tear. Then he hooked his hand behind her knees, pulled her ass to the edge of the bed, spread her legs until she was on full display for him.

Glistening, wet, swollen.

He kneeled in front of her and kissed his way up her shapely calves, her soft thighs, delaying the moment when he would close his mouth around her pussy. She writhed on the bed, her breath coming in short bursts.

"You want my mouth on you, baby?" he murmured against her thigh.

She lifted her head to look at him. "I want all of you everywhere, Nico. Everywhere."

Her words set him on fire, and he brought his mouth to her pussy, dragging his tongue through the moist folds of her sex on his way to her clit. Her hips came up off the bed, and he grabbed tighter to her thighs, keeping her in his grip as he buried his face in her, relishing her sweetness on his tongue. He closed his mouth tight around her clit and sucked until her body bucked under his mouth.

"Oh god, Nico…"

He ran the flat point of his tongue against the engorged nub, fighting the urge to put his fingers inside her, to feel her tighten around them. Driving into her was a kind of occupation. And nothing was going to occupy her but his cock. Not this time.

He moved off her clit, ran his tongue through the crease of her pussy before fucking her with it. His cock didn't need to be inside her to know she was close to coming. He could feel it in the tightening of her thighs, the way her hips moved with the rhythm of his mouth.

He hooked her knees over his shoulders, opening her wider for him. Then he doubled down on her clit, wrapping his mouth around it, sucking as she lifted her hips to meet his mouth. When he sensed her balancing at the precipice, he lapped harder and faster, waiting for the moment when she toppled over, her cries an echo of the waves crashing onto the rock below the bedroom. He kept stroking the tiny bundle of nerves with his tongue as her body shook, the orgasm going on and on as she shuddered against his mouth.

Finally, she lifted her head, looked at him through desire-clouded eyes. "Fuck me now, Nico. I need you inside me."

He growled, moving closer to her so he could position the thick crown of his head against her opening, slick with her come. He took hold of her hips and pulled her to him as he drove into her in one swift movement. Then he put one of her legs on his shoulder, using the position to angle deeper, wanting to own every bit of her, to remind them both that she was his.

"Fuck, Angel," He looked down at her face, the face he'd dreamt of every night since the last time he'd seen her. "You're so fucking beautiful."

Her eyes fluttered open, and he was pulled into their depths, drowning in them as her sex clenched around him. He dragged the length of his shaft in and out of her, the sensation too good to rush. Too good not to. He was already climbing the peak, brought to the edge by the feel of her coming under his tongue, her tight body under his. And she was right there with him, her pussy already gripping him, hips rising off the bed to meet him, hands clenching his ass as she tried to pull him in deeper even as there was nowhere else to go. He already filled every inch of her, felt the tip of his cock hitting the top of her channel, her clit rubbing against him with every thrust.

"Nico..."

"That's right, baby," he said. "Come for me."

The words seemed to set her off. She moved faster, her breath catching in her throat, a soft blush spreading over her body as she climbed with him.

She opened her eyes. "I'm going to come, Nico."

"You are going to come," he said, looking into her eyes. "And I'm going to come with you."

She cried out, digging her nails into his hips and arching her back as she shuddered against him. He let go then, pouring himself into her, making her his all over again.

They lay in bed afterward, her head on his chest. He stroked her hair, listening to her breath turn regular as she drifted off to sleep. It was early afternoon, but she was obviously exhausted, and not just from last night. He'd been so worried about leaving her alone — even with Luca as her bodyguard — but he shouldn't have been. She'd risen to the occasion like the warrior she was. Had stepped into her father's position, cleaned house at Rossi Development and the Boston arm of the Syndicate. Had put aside her grief to do what had to be done.

And there had been grief. He'd been nearby during some of her most vulnerable moments, had seen her break down, bite on her fist to keep from letting someone hear her sobs. That had almost killed him. Every muscle in his body had wanted to go to her, to wrap her in his arms, haul her to his bed where he could make sure no one would ever hurt her again.

Except this time he'd been the one to hurt her. He'd been right when he told her there was no way around it. No way to stay in the picture and keep her safe. But that didn't mean he was off the hook. He had been the source of her tears, her heartbreak. Maybe she could forgive him for it, but he wasn't sure if he could do the same. And what did the future hold for them? Would they ever be free to live without looking over their shoulders? Could they find some semblance of a life together?

They were questions without answers, and he kissed the top of her head, breathing in her scent. It wasn't over, and this time he was under no delusion that she would let him go without her. She would demand to go after Raneiro, to finish the job she'd started with the men who had betrayed him. He would have no choice but to allow it. As much as he wanted to lock her high in a tower — or even here on the island — she was a fighter. She'd find a way to follow.

He couldn't blame her. Her life had been obliterated by the Syndicate. He'd started it when he'd taken her hostage. He would never allow himself to forget that. But he'd given the Syndicate a chance to leave her alone when he'd played dead. Instead they'd come for her in her own home.

And that was something that would not stand.

# 9

She was squeezing oranges for juice the next morning, dawn painting the sky pink and orange, when David walked into the kitchen. He looked sleepy and disheveled, and she suddenly saw him as he'd been when they were kids; a gentle, quiet boy who'd always been quick to grab her hand, kiss her cheek.

"Hey," she said, turning to look at him. "It's early. You sure you don't want to sleep a little later?"

He slid onto one of the bar stools at the island. "It took me awhile to settle down, but I've still been asleep for over twelve hours."

They'd all slept through yesterday, exhausted from everything that had happened and the long drive to Maine. She rinsed her hands and dried them on a towel, then poured coffee into a mug and slid it toward him.

"I know, but it was a long night," she said.

He nodded, took a sip of the coffee. "Can't sleep forever."

She tried not to think about the note of regret in his voice. She looked at the limp bandage on his hand instead. "Want me to clean that up for you?"

He slipped his hand under the counter where it was out of view. "I can do it."

She nodded. "Breakfast will be ready soon."

She turned back to the bowl of eggs she'd been beating for French toast.

"I thought he was dead," David said behind her.

She turned to face him and leaned against the counter. "Me, too."

"So?" His messy hair fell over one cocked eyebrow.

"It's a long story."

"I have time."

She filtered through the information, trying to find the easiest explanation for what had happened — for what was happening now. Trying to find a way to explain it that wouldn't scare him.

"Dante wasn't in charge in LA," she said softly. "Not really."

David drummed his fingers on the counter, a nervous habit from adolescence. "He seemed pretty in charge to me."

"Someone else was behind it. Nico knew it wouldn't end there."

"So he faked his death?" He barked out a sarcastic laugh. "Seems a little melodramatic."

She tamped down her anger. Melodrama wasn't the right word for what Nico had been through during his four months alone, for what Angel had felt when she thought he was dead. But she knew David was hurting, lashing out against the only people still close enough for him to reach.

"Not when Raneiro Donati has a hit out on you."

"Donati?" His forehead crinkled. "I thought he and Nico were tight."

"So did Nico," Angel said. "But apparently Nico's business model hasn't been warmly embraced. Raneiro has had enough."

"So Nico went into hiding?" David asked.

"No." It sounded harsh, and she took a deep breath. "He went underground to protect us, to get a better view on what was happening, who was behind it all."

"And I'm guessing that's pretty clear now?"

She nodded.

"So you're telling me we're targets, too," David said bitterly. "What a surprise."

She crossed her arms over her chest. "What's that supposed to mean?"

"We've been safe for four months, Ange. Four months that Nico Vitale hasn't been around. The first day he comes back someone decides to use us for target practice at the brownstone?" He took a drink of his coffee. "That doesn't sound like a coincidence."

"Nico came back because he heard about the hit on us," Angel said. "The only thing that would have been different if he'd stayed away is that we'd be in the morgue right now."

She turned around, trying to calm down while she added milk to the eggs, beat them together. This wasn't David's fault. It was easier to blame Nico for everything that had happened than to blame their dead father for bringing the Syndicate to their door in the first place, than to blame Angel for refusing to walk away when she had the chance.

"I'm sorry, Ange." David's voice was soft behind her.

"It's okay."

"Hey," he said. She turned to face him. "I'm really sorry."

She nodded.

"I just…"

"What?"

"Will you ever be able to put all this behind you with Nico in the picture?" he asked. "Will you ever be happy — or free — again?"

She was surprised to feel the sting of tears in her eyes. They were questions she didn't ask herself. Answering them meant contemplating a life without Nico, and now that she had him back, she knew that was no life at all.

"I don't know," she said. "I only know that the two most important people in the world are here with me now, and I don't want to live without either one of them. Nico can keep us safe while we figure out a long term plan."

"And after that?"

"I love him, David." She shrugged. "It's all I've got right now."

He nodded, then glanced into the living room. "Where is he?"

"Running," she said. "He likes to jog on the beach in the mornings. It clears his head."

She was putting the first slices of egg-soaked bread on the griddle when Nico entered the house through the doors off the deck. He brought the scent of the sea with him, his hair damp and wavy. His T-shirt was soaked, giving her a perfect view of his sculpted chest. She felt a tightening between her legs as she remembered his dark head there, his magnificent body joining with hers.

"Hey." She cleared her throat. "How was it?"

The corners of his mouth turned up into a knowing smile, like he knew exactly what she'd been thinking. "Amazing."

She wondered if he was talking about the run or something else.

He cut his gaze to David, and his expression grew serious. "Good morning."

"Morning," David said.

Nico held out his hand. "I don't think we've ever met properly."

David looked at his hand a moment before clasping it. "I think you're right."

Nico looked into his eyes. Angel loved him for that, for making sure that David knew he was seen. "Is your room comfortable? Is there anything I can get you?"

David shook his head. "I'm good."

Nico nodded, then came around the island to where Angel was standing over the griddle. She thought he might try to be subtle around David, but she should have known better; Nico would never make apologies for the way he felt about her. He wrapped one arm around her waist and pulled her close, then kissed her tenderly on the mouth.

"Good morning, beautiful." His voice was hoarse.

She smiled. It was real. He was here. "Good morning."

He gave her a squeeze and stepped away. "I'm going to take a quick shower. I'll be down in time for breakfast."

# 10

"Luca's out," Nico said, coming out onto the deck.

They'd eaten a quiet breakfast, every topic of conversation either too weighty or too insignificant for the circumstances. Afterwards, Angel and David had dealt with the dishes while Nico went into his study to call Luca.

"Out?" Angel twisted in the deck chair as he came around to sit next to her. "Out of where?"

"Everywhere," Nico said. "Someone from Rome took over Boston this morning, and all of Luca's permissions have been revoked from the New York servers."

"Is he okay?" Angel asked.

"Luca can take care of himself," Nico said. "He'll see what he can find out and get back to us."

"Raneiro can do what he wants with the Boston territory," Angel said, fighting a tide of anger. "But Rossi Development is a private company, and it belongs to David and me."

"Donati can have it, as far as I'm concerned," David said, his eyes closed against the sun.

"That's easy for you to say. You didn't spend the last four months working there."

He turned his head, shielding his eyes so he could see her. "Working to dismantle it you mean?"

She hid her surprise. She hadn't been sure how much David knew, how much he'd gathered from the business calls she took at the brownstone.

"That's beside the point," she said. "He can't just march in and take over a private company."

"I don't think that's happened," Nico said. "It sounds like the takeover has been Syndicate business only. I'm sure Margaret will handle everything at the office in your absence."

Angel narrowed her eyes. "How do you know about Margaret?"

She had hired Margaret Nolan as her CFO after dumping the corrupt men her father had on the payroll — her "uncle" Frank Morra among them. Margaret had an MBA from Harvard and was about as far removed from the Syndicate as someone could get. She was young, but she'd picked up the business quickly, and Angel had liked that she was a relative outsider. Nico was right; she would hold things together until Angel could figure out what to do about the business.

A smiled played at his lips. "You don't really think I just abandoned you, did you?"

"Wait a minute…" She leaned forward in the chair. "Did you get Margaret to apply for the job?"

"Now you're being paranoid. I'm sure you're more than capable of handling your father's business. I just watched from afar to make sure you were okay."

She settled back into the chair. Protective was one thing. Meddling was another.

"What does it mean?" Angel asked.

"It means we're locked out of Syndicate business," he said. "Luca was our inside man."

"What about Marco and Elia?"

"Luca told them to go dark, too. If Raneiro's on to Luca, it's only a matter of time before he connects the dots to Marco and Elia."

She was hit with a pang of guilt. Luca was like a brother to Nico. He would have done Nico's bidding no matter what. But Marco and Elia had been protecting her, and now they were in danger, too.

Nico reached for her hand. "This isn't your fault. Everyone's a grown up here. They knew what they were getting into."

"What do we do now?" she asked. "We can't hide here forever."

"We have to get to Raneiro. Try to negotiate some kind of exit strategy."

"What kind of exit strategy?" David asked.

"One that will allow you and your sister to live in peace," Nico said.

"Can't we just say we're out?" David asked. "Let them have the Boston territory?"

Nico shook his head. "There's only one way out of the Syndicate in a situation like this, and it's not a resignation letter."

"So they're going to kill us?" David asked.

Alarm rang through Angel's body at the calm acceptance in his voice. It was the medication. Making him apathetic. Making him too tired to fight for his life. He just needed to get well. Then he'd want to live again.

"They're going to try," Nico said. "But I know Raneiro; there has to be something he wants more than making an example out of us. Out of me."

"Like what?" Angel asked.

"I don't know," Nico said. "But I'm going to find out."

# 11

"I can't leave David here alone," Angel said. "I just can't."

Nico sat next to her on the bed and took her hand. "What's going on? Talk to me."

She drew in a breath. "He's just… he's not well, that's all. He's in therapy and he's on medication and I just… I can't leave him by himself."

Nico rubbed his thumb against her palm, wishing he could take away all her sadness, all her worry. Wishing he could make things easy and beautiful for her. But that was for later — after he'd dealt with Raneiro. After he'd removed every threat to her life. Then he'd do whatever it took to see that she got what she deserved.

"So that means we take him with us or we find someone to stay with him," Nico said. If Angel said David wasn't up to staying alone, then they wouldn't leave him alone. But based on everything she said — not to mention the things Nico had observed for himself — David was too fragile to accompany them on what would undoubtedly be a dangerous bid for their freedom. Nico was already worried about keeping Angel safe; introducing David into the mix was pushing it, especially in David's obviously traumatized state. "I'm thinking he'd be better off here."

"I agree," Angel said. "But it's not like we have a lot of people on our side, and the three people we still trust are in hiding."

Nico paced to the balcony doors, looked out over the ocean. Luca would come to Maine if Nico asked, would stay with David as long as was necessary. But they might need Luca in the field, and Marco and Elia, too. Those kinds of resources were hard to come buy — especially now. Nico couldn't afford to have his best men playing checkers on an island when he and Angel were the subject of a high priority hit by Raneiro Donati. He ran through the very short list of people he would trust with Angel's beloved brother and came to a stop at one name.

"I think I might know someone," he said.

"Who?"

"Sara."

Sara Falco was a hacker Nico had recruited form the FBI training program. She was the best they'd ever had, and Nico had hand-picked her to help them dig through a mountain of raw data to find David in Los Angeles. Angel had seemed to like her.

Angel lifted an eyebrow. "Sara Falco? Won't the Syndicate get suspicious if she takes off right after they banish Luca?"

"Sara hasn't been with the family since June," Nico said.

Angel couldn't hide her surprise. "What do you mean? Where has she been?"

"Went into private consulting," Nico said.

"Because of what happened with David?"

Sara had been in an adjoining building during the rescue in LA, monitoring the operation through a live feed connected to body cams and mics on Nico and the men. Nico hadn't been able to talk to her afterward, but Luca insinuated that the operation — and the resulting deaths — had been traumatic for her. She'd had the same training as the men in the family, but she'd always been behind the scenes on her computer. LA had been her first experience up close and personal with violence, and Nico suspected she was too gentle for it to sit well.

"I'm sure that was part of it," Nico said. "But in my experience, those kinds of decisions are usually a long time coming."

Angel chewed her bottom lip. "Do you trust her enough to bring her here?"

It was a legitimate question. Even Luca didn't know about the island. But Sara had tactical training. She was tough, but she also had the tender touch David would need in Angel's absence. And it's not like they were overflowing with possibilities.

"Do you?" he asked.

"I think so," Angel said.

The fear on her face tore at his insides. She never showed that kind of fear for herself. It was always directed at David's safety, or toward Nico, who hadn't realized he missed having someone to worry about him until he'd met Angel.

He crossed back to the bed, took her hand, kissed her palm and pulled her up so he could take her face in his hands. He lowered his lips to hers, pouring all his feeling into the kiss, gently sweeping her mouth with his tongue until she was like liquid heat against him.

"I love you, Angel. It's been a long time since I've been able to say it, but I need you to know it."

She touched his face. "I love you, too. Just promise you'll never leave me again."

He felt a chill as she said the words. He wouldn't leave voluntarily, but he didn't know how things would play out with someone like Raneiro. And Nico wouldn't make promises to her that he wouldn't keep.

He ran his hands up her shoulders. "I won't willingly leave you again."

A shadow drifted in front of her eyes, and her slender throat rippled as she swallowed the words. She wouldn't beg for reassurance. She was a better woman than that.

He dropped a gentle kiss on her mouth, savoring the velvety softness of her lips under his. "You should take a nap."

She ran her hands under his T-shirt, up the muscled peaks and valleys of his chest. "I was thinking of a better use of this time than sleep."

He groaned. "If I had my way, I'd keep you naked in my bed all day just so I could do wicked things to your body."

She smiled. "Sounds good to me."

He chuckled. "Tell you what: get in bed, get a little nap. You're going to need it. I'm going to call Sara, take care of some things. I'll be back in an hour."

She kissed him, slipped her tongue in his mouth, ran a hand down the rigid bulge of his cock. "If you're sure…"

He moaned, stepping away with effort. "I'm not at all sure. But it's what has to be done."

She stripped off her T-shirt and jeans while he watched. She wasn't wearing underclothes, and she slipped naked between the sheets. Christ. How was he supposed to concentrate knowing she was waiting for him like that?

"Hurry back," she said.

He left the room before he could change his mind.

# 12

Nico left late the next night to meet Sara at the dock. It had been a busy two days of calls and plans, most of them made by Nico behind the closed door of his office while Angel kept David company. David wasn't crazy about the idea of staying with someone he didn't know, but he'd finally admitted it was the only possible option given Angel's refusal to leave him alone. She understood. It's not like she liked leaving him. What if she was remembering Sara wrong? What if Sara wasn't as gentle or calm or intelligent as Angel recollected during the dark days in LA prior to David's rescue?

But any doubts she had disappeared the minute Sara stepped into the house. Her hair was the color of an old penny, wet from the light rain that had started after dinner. Her clothes were rumpled, and she looked tired — probably from the long day of travel -- but still, her face broke into a smile as soon as she saw Angel.

They embraced fiercely, and Angel realized she hadn't seen Sara since Nico's funeral. Angel had been a wreck, her memories of that time muffled under a thick blanket of pain she didn't dare remove. But Sara had been there. She remembered that. Sara had been there, and she'd been kind and tender in her support of Angel.

"Thank you so much for coming," Angel said when they finally pulled apart.

Sara shook her head. "No thanks necessary. I'm just…" She cut an incredulous glance at Nico that left no doubt she'd been in the dark about Nico's fake death. "I'm just so glad he's alive."

Angel smiled. "Me, too."

Sara turned her attention to David, standing quietly near the couch. "You must be David." She crossed the room to shake his hand without so much as glancing at his bandage. "I hope you like checkers, because I'm fucking lousy at chess."

David cracked a faint smile. "I can do checkers."

Sara returned his smile. "Awesome."

"You must be hungry," Nico said. "Why don't you let Angel get you a drink while I heat you up some food? We have leftover clam sauce, my mother's recipe."

The words caused a flash of memory; the first night she'd been alone with Nico in his New York apartment, the food she'd assumed he'd ordered, the lick of desire between her legs when he'd dropped his mouth to her neck while she'd tried to rinse her plate in the sink.

So not take out after all. How was it that he could still surprise her?

"Sounds wonderful," Sara said.

"What can I get you to drink?" Angel asked.

"I'd love a glass of wine if you have it," she said. "Help me settle down a bit before bed."

Nico went to the kitchen to heat up the food while Angel poured them glasses of wine — all except for David who wasn't supposed to drink while he was on his meds.

"How have you been?" Angel asked, settling onto the couch next to Sara.

"I've been good," Sara said. She took a drink of the wine, nodded appreciatively.

"Not with the family anymore?"

Sara shook her head, stared down at the ruby liquid in her glass. "After LA…" She glanced at David. "After what happened to David, and then Nico and the others… I just don't think it's for me." She laughed drily. "Guess I should have stayed with the Feds where I could hide behind my computer."

Angel took her hand and gave it a squeeze. "You don't have to apologize for your humanity."

Sara nodded.

"So what are you doing now?" Angel asked. "Or is it top secret?"

Sara shook her head. "Nothing that exciting, I'm afraid. I'm in corporate security, working freelance for a multinational company that needs extra security."

"That sounds interesting," Angel said.

Sara laughed. "It's not. But I'm starting to think interesting is overrated."

Angel smiled. "I'm starting to agree with you."

Nico handed Sara a plate of steaming pasta. "Can I get you anything else?"

"This is great, thanks," she said, setting down her wine glass so she could dig into the food. She took a bite, closed her eyes and groaned. "Oh, my god… this is amazing."

"I'll give your compliments to the chef," Nico said.

Angel hooked her thumb at him. "He's the chef."

"Well, he can keep the job as far as I'm concerned," Sara said, tucking a piece of hair behind her ear and going in for another bite. "What about you?" she asked Angel. "How's the corporate world treating you?"

Angel chose her words carefully. "It's not exactly fun," she admitted. "But it's giving me a platform to accomplish some important things. Although… I'm not sure about any of that now."

Sara's expression turned serious. "I heard about Boston. I'm sorry. That must have been scary after everything you and David have already been through."

Angel took a drink of her wine. "It was."

But even as she said it, she didn't know if it was true. Had she been scared? At the time, a kind of cold fury had settled over her, all of her intellectual resources focused on getting David out alive. Had she changed so much that she couldn't even feel fear anymore? Had she become so distanced from her old self that emotion had been replaced by calculation?

They talked a little about the island, about the logistics of getting groceries delivered from Ed and his wife, about the generator that turned on automatically if the power went out and the short wave radio they could use to contact Ed if the phones went down.

The conversation made Angel nervous. Was she really about to do this? To leave her brother with someone she hardly knew? To endanger her own safety again by going after Raneiro Donati?

But she didn't have a choice. David would never be safe as long as Raneiro and those who followed him were out there. They had plenty of money stashed in offshore accounts, the proceeds of the very large trust left to them by their father. David would be okay no matter what, and whatever happened to her, he would be better off with Raneiro out of the picture.

She'd gone through a second glass of wine by the time Sara finished her food. Nico cleaned up in the kitchen while Angel took Sara upstairs to one of the guest rooms.

"Wow," Sara said. "This is gorgeous."

Like all of the bedrooms in the house, it faced the private beach, a set of French doors leading to a balcony that jutted out over the rocky shoreline.

"I can't tell you how much I appreciate this," Angel said. "David is..." She took a deep breath. "He's fragile right now. On medication for PTSD and depression. I couldn't leave him alone."

Sara gave her a quick hug. "I understand. I'll keep a close eye on him, I promise."

"You just have to watch his meds," Angel said. "Make sure he's taking the right amount. And he needs company, even when it seems like he wants to be left alone." She felt guilty as she said it. She hadn't been a great example in Boston, that's for sure. "I'll go over all of it tomorrow before Nico and I leave."

"I'm sure David and I will be fast friends," Sara said.

"And you were able to get the time off work?" Angel asked.

"I work remotely most of the time anyway," she said. "And I'll be sure to route any of my activity through more than one foreign IP."

"Great." Angel had no worries about Sara on that account. She was one of the best hackers the FBI had ever recruited. "There are towels and stuff in the bathroom. Just make yourself at home."

"Thank you," Sara smiled. "I just wish we had more time to visit before you and Nico leave."

"We'll catch up on the back end," Angel said. She was surprised to find she really wanted to do it. She'd been too isolated for too long, and Sara was one of the few people who understood the world she'd become part of.

"I'm going to hold you to that," Sara said.

"I'm counting on it." Angel was almost to the door when she remembered something. "I've been wondering…"

Were she and Sara close enough that she could ask? She wasn't sure.

Sara smiled. "About Luca and me?"

Angel nodded. "You don't have to tell me."

"There's not much to tell," she said, looking down at her hands. "It never really went anywhere."

"Because of you or because of him?" Angel asked.

"Both?" It was a question and a statement. "I don't know, Angel. Luca's so… closed off, you know?"

She did know. She counted Luca as one of her closest friends, and yet she knew very little about him beyond his difficult childhood and the fact that Nico had stepped in to offer him a chance at something better.

"He had a rough start," Angel said.

"I figured as much," Sara said. "But I'm just at a place in my life where I want to be with someone who's capable of being with me, you know?"

Angel smiled. "You deserve that."

"Thanks," Sara said. "My mom always says everything turns out the way it's supposed to. I'm hoping she's right."

"That makes two of us," Angel said.

# 13

They woke up early the next day and gathered their things. Angel was glad she hadn't had the heart to throw out any of Nico's clothes when she thought he was dead; they both had enough to work with from the dresser drawers of the Maine house, and they were packed and ready to go by ten am.

Nico took Sara around the house, showing her the boiler and fuse box, the security system, and everything else she would need to know to run things in their absence. Angel found David on the beach, sitting on one of the big rocks that looked out across the water.

The sun was high in a cloudless sky as she picked her way across the sand, but the wind blowing in off the water was chilly. It wouldn't be long before winter arrived, and she couldn't help wondering where they would all be when it did; would they be alive and well here or somewhere else? Would they have struck a deal with Raneiro that would allow them to live in peace? Or would their numbers be smaller, culled by the vicious men who worked on behalf of Raneiro Donati and the Syndicate?

She was being morbid. They'd come through too much together. She couldn't afford to believe in anything but an outcome in which they were all safe and sound. She didn't know what it would mean for them, but she had stashed the trust from their father safely offshore. She and David would have plenty of money to live comfortably if she made it out alive.

"Hey," she said, when she finally reached David.

He didn't look at her. "Hey."

"You okay?" she asked.

"What do you want me to say?"

"What do you mean?" she asked.

"Do you want me to tell you the truth? Or do you want me to tell you what you want to hear so you can leave without feeling guilty?"

The words stung. Had she given David reason to think she didn't want the truth from him?

"I want the truth, David. I always want the truth from you."

He turned to look at her. "Then no, I'm not okay."

"What's wrong?"

His laugh was short and brittle. "What's wrong?"

She sighed. "I mean, I know this isn't ideal, but I thought we'd reached a workable solution."

"A workable solution? Do you hear yourself, Ange?" he asked softly. He continued without waiting for her to answer. "Are you really so shut down that you don't see this for what it is?"

She shook her head, looked out over the water. "I don't know what you're talking about."

"I'm talking about you taking off with Nico to face a vicious murderer. One who wants to kill you. I'm talking about you leaving me here with someone I don't know while you risk your life, when you're basically the only thing I have left to live for."

"Don't say that," she hissed.

"Look at me, Ange." She did, because he was her brother, and even though the pain in his eyes tore her apart, she couldn't not look at him when he needed to be seen. "It's true. I need you. You're all I have left. And you're acting like this is some kind of… vacation or something. Like there isn't a possibility you won't be back."

"I'll be back," she said quietly.

"You don't know that."

She took his hand, looked into his eyes, the same eyes she'd been looking into since she was four years old. "I'll be back, David. I'm doing this for us."

"Do you really believe that?" he asked.

She pulled her hand away, hurt by his implication. "Don't you?"

"I think there's more to it than that."

"Like what?"

"I think this is a continuation of what you were doing in Boston. I think you're angry. Angrier than you want to admit. And I think you want revenge at any cost."

She stood, paced a few feet away, looked back at him as the familiar rage rose inside her. "And what's so wrong with that?" she asked. "Don't we deserve a little justice?"

He shook his head. "It's not about that."

She held out her palms. "Then what's it about?"

"It's about *living,* Ange. Isn't that what you've been telling me I need to do?"

A hand seemed to squeeze her lungs, and she dragged in a breath, the truth of his words warring with the story she'd been telling herself. He didn't understand. He'd been able to hide in a drug-induced stupor. She'd had to get up every morning, keep moving. She knew all about what it took to live. And the way she'd been living — without Nico, face-to-face with the Syndicate's despicable income streams, in fear of her safety and David's — well, it fucking sucked.

"Don't you think I want to live?" she asked him. "I want to live as much as anybody. But what I've been doing isn't living, and I can't keep doing it. *We* can't keep doing it. Especially now. They've given us no choice, David."

"You could let Nico go," he said. "Let him and Luca handle it."

"I can't do that," she said. "This is my fight, too."

She didn't say the other thing: that she couldn't be without Nico again. That being without him wasn't living. That letting him go after Raneiro in the name of her safety while she stayed safe on the island was something she couldn't live with. She didn't know if David would understand the depth of her feelings for Nico, the way his heart had intertwined with hers so completely that she was sure it would stop beating if he were ripped from her again. Maybe going with him was no guarantee of his safety, but she was going to stay

by his side from here on out. Whatever the future held for them —
life, death — they would face it together.

David's shoulders sagged in resignation. "Then do what you
have to do, Ange."

She walked back to where he stood. "I'll be back. And then
we'll start over, I promise."

He stood, wrapping her in his arms. When had he gotten taller
than her?

"I love you, Ange. And I need you. Just don't forget it," he
said.

"Never." She squeezed him tighter.

She closed her eyes as memories flashed in her mind: David's
scared face the first day of Kindergarten when she'd walked him to
his classroom. David holding the flashlight under her covers so she
could read to him in the dark. David wiping her tears when she
thought Nico was gone forever.

"Love you, loser," she said.

He choked out a laugh. She tried to memorize the sound of it.
Tried to banish the feeling that she wouldn't be back to hear it again.

# 14

Ed was waiting when they got to the dock. He took their bags, and Angel and Sara embraced while David stood silently by. They hadn't been around each other enough for Nico to expect David to like him. They didn't even know each other. But Nico needed to do his part to set the record straight before he left with Angel.

He clasped a hand on David's back and turned away from the women. "I'm going to keep her safe," Nico said. He might not be able to guarantee his own safety, but he would get Angel home to her brother even if it killed him. "You can count on it."

"I don't see how you can promise that," David said.

Nico looked in his eyes. "I am promising. And I don't make promises lightly."

"Okay," David said.

Nico considered his next words. "I know we haven't had a chance to get to know each other, and I know you have every reason to despise me. But I love your sister with everything I am. Her safety matters more to me than my own life, and since you matter to her, that means your safety matters that much to me, too. If there were another way, I'd take it. But you and I both know she won't stay."

He hesitated, then nodded.

"And you have to do your part, too," Nico said.

David looked surprised. "My part?"

"You have to get well," Nico said. "You have to show her that you want to stay alive, because right now, she's living in fear that you don't, and I'm not sure she'd be able to make it without you. She needs you. Do you understand?"

"She needs me?" David asked.

"That's right," Nico said. "She's been carrying all of this on her shoulders while you get well, but she can't do it forever, and she can't do it without you. So take this time to regroup. Take your meds. Sleep and talk to Sara. Pull it together so that when she comes back you can be here for her."

He didn't say the other thing lingering in the back of his mind; that if he didn't make it out alive, Angel would need her brother even more.

David's nod was slower this time, like he was really thinking about what Nico said. "Okay."

Nico clasped his back. "Good."

He said a quick goodbye to Sara and got in the boat while Angel exchanged a few words with her brother. Her eyes glistened with unshed tears, but she kept her chin up, even tried to smile as Ed pulled away from the dock. She waved until they turned back toward the house.

Nico put his arm around her. "They'll be okay."

She nodded, but he couldn't be sure she believed him.

They sped across the water and were back in Bass Harbor well before noon. After some quick instructions to Ed — including a weekly grocery drop to the island — he and Angel made their way up to the parking lot where they'd left Luca's SUV. It wasn't ideal. Nico had no way of knowing if Raneiro was searching for the vehicle. But it was a chance they'd have to take until they could get some clean papers and a new car.

"Are we going to the Hudson Valley house?" Angel asked when he got on the highway heading south.

"The Hudson Valley house burned to the ground a month after we rescued David."

He didn't look at her as he said it. The pain of losing the historic house — the one place where he most felt his mother's presence — was still too raw. He'd loved having Angel there last fall, had hoped to bring her back, to share the history of his family summers there with her. In some of his wildest dreams, he even thought they might have children who would grow up there one day.

"Burned to the…" she didn't say anything for a long minute. "What happened?"

"Electrical short, they said."

"They?"

"The fire marshall."

"Were they right?" she asked.

"Probably not."

She reached across the console and took his free hand. The feel of her small hand over his, trying to offer him comfort after everything he'd brought to her door, almost undid him.

"I'm so, so sorry, Nico," she said softly.

He nodded. "Me, too."

"Why would someone do that?"

"To make sure I had nowhere to go," he said simply.

"You can rebuild it," she suggested. "When this is all over."

"Maybe."

The task in front of them wasn't a small one. Getting out of the Syndicate with a free pass to a new life was unheard of after a hit had been taken out. The hit meant you'd already crossed the point of no return. That you'd betrayed them or fucked up so bad they needed to make an example of you. Letting you go then was a show of weakness, and the only way Raneiro would be willing to risk a show of weakness is if taking another course was so valuable that the upsides outweighed it.

And Nico wasn't fooling himself; there were few things worth a show of weakness to Raneiro Donati.

He was glad when Angel changed the subject.

"So where are we going?" she asked.

"Albany."

"Albany?"

He nodded. "There's a small international airport there. The city is low key but big enough to get lost in for a little while. We'll get a hotel, buy a cheap phone, and call Raneiro. Then we'll figure out what's next."

He took them up through the Berkshires and into Vermont before cutting back down into New York. He was steering clear of Boston, and while he wasn't crazy about the tolls — toll booths always had cameras — there was no way to get to New York without them that wouldn't involve miles of backroads.

They stopped once for dinner and twice for gas and arrived in Albany just after sunset. The city was old and gritty, populated by brick buildings that had been standing since the early 1900s — some of them even longer — and bordered by the Hudson River in the east. He took the turnoff for the airport and pulled up to the ticket machine for long term parking.

"I thought we were getting a hotel," Angel said, waking up in the passenger seat as the lights from the parking lot shone into the front seat.

"We are." He navigated the car toward a spot farthest from the terminal. "But we need to ditch this car first."

They removed their bags from the backseat and left the ticket on the dash. Then he led Angel away from the terminal, not wanting to be caught on one of the airport's security cameras. He walked backwards, looking for a cab leaving without any passengers, and finally flagged one just before they hit the main road leading away from the airport.

The cabbie dropped them a couple of miles away at a sleazy motel. A hundred dollar bill let them slide without ID. Nico wasn't crazy about bringing Angel there even for a night; he wanted her to have the best of everything. Wanted her sleeping on silk sheets and waited on hand and foot. But that would have to come later, after he'd secured her safety. For now, they needed to stay under the radar, and that meant avoiding the use of their real names.

"I'm sorry about this," he said, setting their bags down in the tiny room.

She looked confused. "About what?"

"This… room," he said, looking around.

She walked toward him, put her arms around his neck, looked into his eyes. "I don't care about the room, Nico."

She stood on tip-toe, touched her lips to his, slipped her tongue in his mouth. His cock immediately responded, standing at attention like it always did when she touched him. He couldn't remember what it was like to be touched by someone else, to be kissed by someone else. He hoped he would never have to be reminded. He only wanted her. Today and forever.

Her mouth on his. Her hands on his body.

She took his lower lip between her teeth and tugged until he groaned.

"Work now, play later," she said.

He sighed. "Tease."

They left the room and walked to a nearby diner with sticky vinyl seats and slightly dim fluorescent lighting. After they ate, they bought four cheap Tracphones at a gas station and walked to the edge of a vacant lot. It wasn't the greatest neighborhood, but they needed privacy. Nico was armed. They would have to take their chances.

"You sure you want to do this?" Angel asked when he booted up the phone.

"We don't have a choice," he said.

She opened her mouth like she wanted to say something, then closed it.

"What?" he asked.

"I was going to say we could run. Just get David and run."

"But?"

She shook her head. "I don't want to run."

He smiled at her through the darkness. "Me, either."

He opened the phone and dialed the number he'd memorized after the death of his parents. Raneiro answered on the second ring.

"Who are you and how did you get this number?"

The voice almost stopped Nico cold. It was the voice of his mentor and friend. The voice of the man who had been like a father to him after his own father had been murdered by Carlo Rossi. But it was also the voice of a cold-blooded killer. A kid who'd grown up on the mean streets of Sicily and now gave orders to the most vicious men in the world.

"It's Nico," he said. "We have two minutes before I disconnect this call."

He couldn't be sure Raneiro had the kind of tech savvy on staff to trace the call after the fact. But Raneiro had money. Lots of money. And money would buy any kind of knowledge. It was better to be safe.

"Nico..." He felt a twinge of satisfaction at the note of surprise in Raneiro's voice. "Where are you?"

"You know I'm not going to tell you that, Nero. Cut the shit. Tell me what you want."

A low chuckle unspooled from the other end of the phone. "Always straight and to the point, Nico. I have always liked that about you."

"So?" Nico prompted.

"What do *you* want, Nico?" Raneiro's voice was cold now, all hint of affection gone.

"I want out. For Angelica Rossi, her brother, and me. A free pass."

"Nothing is free in this life, Nico. Didn't your father teach you that before Carlo Rossi put a bullet in his brain?"

Nico reigned in his temper. He had been groomed by Raneiro, and he knew all the older man's tricks. Raneiro was baiting him, trying to throw him off balance by appealing to emotion.

"Then tell me what you want as a trade," Nico said.

"Some things can't be bought or traded," Raneiro said. "You let a woman infiltrate your mind, Nico, your heart. Now you pay the price, and so does she. The east coast is in shambles. I've given you more than enough time to rectify the situation. The only thing left is to make an example of you."

Nico looked at the time ticking on the phone's display. He had nine seconds left before he had to disconnect the call.

"Everyone has a price, Nero. You taught me that. There's something you want more than you want to make an example out of me. Tell me what it is and you'll have it."

1:57... 1:58... 1:59...

"Phone me again tomorrow at the same time," Raneiro said.

Nico disconnected the call, then crushed the phone under his foot.

# 15

They didn't speak about Raneiro again that night. Instead, they went back to the hotel and made love into the morning. It was a strange kind of decadence — setting aside the outside world, the contract on their lives, the possibility that they wouldn't live to have a future together — to lose themselves in each other. For a few hours, the dingy motel room faded to nothing. There was only Nico's arms around her, his body sinking into hers while she cried his name, his mouth on her sex while she writhed in his hands. There was only his smooth skin, the defined angles of his body, his mouth devouring her like he would never have enough.

They fell asleep just before the sun came up and roused themselves around noon to get food. They walked the opposite direction from the diner, not wanting to be seen too often in the same place, and stopped at a hole in the wall that served tacos and burritos from a walk-up window. They took their food to a small table shielded by an umbrella. Angel was unwrapping her first taco when she finally asked the question that had been hovering in the back of her mind.

"What if Raneiro doesn't want to trade?"

"He will," Nico said. "A man like Raneiro always wants something."

"What if it's something we can't get him?" she asked.

Nico took a long drink of his water. "We'll have to find a way to get it."

"And then what?" she asked. "We do what he wants and let him walk away?"

Nico shook his head. "I'm not sure anyone 'lets' Raneiro do anything. He does what he wants. The rest of us make allowances accordingly."

"What about all that he's done?" Angel had to work to keep her voice calm. "What about bankrolling David's kidnapping? Shooting at me in my own house? Forcing you underground for four months? He just gets away with it all?"

He took her hand. "Getting out of the Syndicate alive after all that's happened is a best case scenario, Angel. Expecting to exact revenge along the way would be pushing it, even for me."

She pulled her hand away, the food turning in her stomach. "He ruined our lives," she said. "David will never be the same."

*And neither will I.* She didn't say it out loud, but it was true. When she'd come back from London after her father's death, she'd been devastated by the truth about her father, by everything that had happened with Nico. But it was all recoverable back then. She was going to start over, figure out a plan to move on with her life.

Then Raneiro sanctioned the attacks on the Vitale family. Angel had stepped in to help Nico, and David had become a casualty of the turf war. His kidnapping and mutilation, followed by what had felt like the very real death of Nico, had flipped a switch inside her, changing something fundamental about who she was. She would never be able to get back all those old parts of herself, and even if Raneiro let them go, they would be looking over their shoulders their whole lives.

"I know that," Nico said. "But I think we need to be smart here, because it's going to come down to life or revenge. I know what I want most. Do you?"

She turned her face away, not wanting to answer the question.

"You're going to have to answer, Angel. If not for me, than for yourself."

She was still thinking about the question when they left the motel room later that night armed with the second of their four Tracphones. Life or revenge. She wanted life, didn't she? A life with Nico? One where David was safe and happy? Did it matter if Raneiro paid for his crimes against them? The answer should have come easy.

They walked toward a McDonald's this time, keeping up their pattern of changing locations. She wasn't sure such remedial measures would matter if Raneiro ever tracked them to this part of Albany, but she couldn't argue that it was worth a shot.

Nico pulled the phone from his pocket. He was starting to dial when she put a hand on his arm. "Wait."

"What is it?" he asked.

"I want to hear what he says."

He hesitated, then nodded. "I'll keep the phone between us."

"Thanks."

He dialed and angled the phone out from his ear so she would hear it ringing. A moment later Raneiro's voice came on the line. She had a flash of him the time he'd checked up on her in Boston: cold eyes, expensive suit, the kind of apathy that told her he wasn't afraid to bet it all, even if he lost. A man with a lot to lose who wouldn't mind losing it.

"It's me," Nico said.

"I've always appreciated your punctuality," Raneiro said.

"You taught me that it was rude to keep people waiting."

Angel was surprised by the warmth of the laughter that made its way across the miles. "So I did, Nico. So I did."

"Did you think about it?" Nico asked. "About what you want in exchange for our freedom?"

"There is little that's more important to me than my position in the Syndicate — and in pursuing opportunities for its growth. Letting you and Miss Rossi go will make it harder to maintain respect within the ranks."

"What is it you want us to do?" Nico asked.

Angel pulled back from the phone and looked at Nico. Raneiro was making it clear that there was nothing he wanted as much as he wanted to make an example of them.

Nico shook his head and held up a finger, indicating that she should wait.

"As I've said - " Raneiro started.

"You said there was 'little' that's more important to you," Nico interrupted. "Not nothing."

"Astute as always," Raneiro said. Angel could almost see the smile on his face, and then she understood; he was fucking with them. There was something he wanted, but he wanted to make them sweat before revealing it.

"Just tell me what it will take," Nico forced the words out through clenched teeth.

"Well, there is one thing…"

"I'm waiting."

"It's an impossible task," Raneiro said. "Especially for you and Miss Rossi, given your lack of recent tactical experience."

"It didn't seem to slow me down when I was putting a bullet in your man's head back in Boston," Nico said.

The phone went silent, and for a minute, Angel thought Raneiro had hung up. Finally he spoke.

"I've been looking into a new revenue stream," Raneiro said. "It's quite competitive, and a certain data file held by a certain someone would go a long way toward getting my foot in the door."

"Hire a hacker," Nico said. "They're a dime a dozen now."

Raneiro sighed. "I'm afraid this is more complicated. This particular file is reputed to be held on an external hard drive that is impossible to access, even for the best."

"Reputed to be held?" Nico repeated.

"Well, yes. You see, I don't know exactly where it is."

"Then how are we supposed to get it?" Nico asked.

"I can point you in the right direction, given our history. Give you a little head start, so to speak. It's your problem beyond that."

Nico pulled the Tracphone away from his ear to look at the time: four-minutes, thirty-nine seconds. Way longer than their two minute limit. Angel saw his frustration in the clench of his jaw, the fire crackling in his eyes.

"Tell me what you know," he said into the phone.

"The data is in the possession of Sean Murdock."

She met Nico's gaze, saw her own confusion reflected there.

"The software guy?" Nico said.

"I'm afraid Mr. Murdock is quite a bit more than a 'software guy', Nico. But then, I imagine you'll find that out once you get to work."

"What am I looking for exactly?" Nico asked. "A guy like Murdock must have countless proprietary files."

"The file you're looking for will be labeled Darknet."

"And that's it?" Nico asked. "Bring you the file, and we get a free pass to walk away from the Syndicate?"

"You have my word," Raneiro said. "This opportunity does, however, have a time limit."

"What is it?"

"Let's call it a month," Raneiro said.

"I'll call you to arrange the drop."

"Fine. And Nico?"

"Yes?"

"Don't be late."

## 16

"So Raneiro is getting into some new kind of black market business," Angel said as she slipped on her jeans the next morning.

Nico laced up his shoes. "It's the only thing I can think of given the name of the file."

They'd gone straight from the phone call with Raneiro to a Best Buy where they'd purchased an iPad with cash. They spent the next two hours sitting on the bed in the motel room, searching the word "Darknet" and reading everything they could find on Sean Murdock. It hadn't taken them long to find information about both, and Darknet quickly revealed itself as a series of online marketplaces used to buy and sell everything from drugs to the worst kind of porn, all of it transacted with Bitcoin for maximum anonymity.

"I just don't get why this is such a big deal to Raneiro," she said. "It's not like the Syndicate is new to the black market."

Nico stood. "I don't know any more than you. It could be anything."

"You think there's something on the file that he can sell?" Angel asked.

"Or something he can use as leverage. You saw the data."

She thought about everything they'd read on Sean Murdock. Raneiro had been right; Murdock was more than just a software guy.

It was true that he'd founded the richest software company in the world, one with reach into every country and every corporation in America. But he'd also started a multi-billion dollar philanthropic organization that donated hundreds of millions of dollars to causes ranging from clean water initiatives in third world countries to orphanages in Southeast Asia. The guy owned an airline and a record label, and was a partner in start up initiatives too numerous to count. He was young (thirty-six years old), single, and without any living family. And while they'd found hundreds of pictures with him at red carpet events draped with the Supermodel of the Hour, relatively little was known about his personal life.

"It's just a weird trade," Angel said, pulling her hair into a ponytail. "What if we give him what he wants and he kills us anyway?" The question had been digging into her mind ever since last night's phone call.

"We'll figure something out — some kind of guarantee," Nico said. "Let's just take it a step at a time for now."

"I'm still not sold on the idea of letting him off the hook," she said.

"We don't have to decide anything now." He holstered his gun to his body, then slipped on his jacket to hide the weapon. "Ready?"

She nodded.

They left the motel and headed for a questionable looking Chinese restaurant they'd spotted while walking the neighborhood. It was open at all hours of the day, the lights so dim Angel almost couldn't see in through the windows. They found Luca in a booth at the back. She didn't know what she expected; for Luca to be harried? To be scared? But he looked just the same, as calm and unreadable as ever.

He and Nico embraced. Luca bent to kiss Angel's cheek, and they all slid into the red pleather booth.

"Thanks for coming," Nico said.

"No thanks necessary, boss."

Nico took a drink of the water glass on the table. "I don't think I'm the boss anymore."

"New York will always belong to you as far as I'm concerned," Luca said.

Nico nodded. "Are you okay?"

"Fine," Luca said. "I was prepared for this eventuality, same as you."

Angel looked from Nico to Luca, wondering what he meant. "What eventuality are we talking about here?"

Luca pushed a thick manila envelope across the table. "This one."

Nico opened the envelope and withdrew a handful of documents. Angel watched as he flipped threw them — passports, driver's licenses, social security cards, even a couple of credit cards and a thick stack of cash. Angel reached for the driver's license with her picture.

"Juliet Moore," she murmured. She looked at Luca. "Where did you get these?"

Luca cut his gaze to Nico.

"He got them from a safe deposit box in Newburgh," Nico said, "where I've been keeping them in case a situation like this should arise."

She dropped the license. "In case Raneiro took out a hit on me, you mean?"

"Angel…"

"Did you know this would happen if you disappeared?" she asked.

"I couldn't be sure," he said. "I thought it might happen no matter what I did, so I decided to play it safe. There are new documents for David, too, if he needs them."

She didn't know what to say. On the one hand, it was weird to think of Nico making all these arrangements while she worked in Boston the last few months, completely oblivious to the things that were already in motion. But while she'd been careful to stash cash offshore for her and David, she hadn't thought about securing false documents, something they would need if they wanted to move freely.

She looked at Nico. "Thank you."

"You're welcome." He put everything back in the envelope, then looked at Luca. "What did you learn about Murdock?"

"Same as you," Luca said. "Billionaire playboy, no family, surface do-gooder…."

Angel met his eyes. "Surface do-gooder?"

Luca turned his water glass in his hand. "I did a little digging. There are rumors in certain circles."

"What kind of rumors?" Angel asked.

"Rumors that Murdock might have… off the book interests."

"Like what?" Nico asked.

"You name it," Luca said. "Drugs, trafficking, illegal weapons… but it's nothing substantial, nothing that can be proven, and a guy with Murdock's wealth is a target for that kind of speculation, so I'd say take it with a grain of salt until we have evidence to the contrary."

Nico nodded.

Luca hesitated. "There is one thing that might help."

"What is it?" Nico asked.

"Murdock had a close friend, someone he's known since they were kids together in Dublin. Guy's name is Desmond McDermott, and he was Murdock's right hand man until about a year ago when he disappeared from Murdock's life."

"What do you mean 'disappeared'?" Angel asked.

Luca shrugged. "Stopped showing up with Murdock at events. Wasn't seen with Murdock in public. To know what a big deal it is, you have to understand that they were virtually inseparable. Murdock called McDermott his bodyguard, but everyone who knew them said they were like brothers."

"You think they had a falling out? That McDermott had him eliminated?"

"The falling out? Maybe," Luca said. "But McDermott is alive and well and living in Rome."

Angel sat up straighter. "Rome?" It's where Raneiro Donati and the Syndicate were headquartered.

Luca nodded.

"That's unfortunate," Nico muttered.

Luca laughed. "That's one word for it."

"You think McDermott might talk to us?" Nico asked.

"I don't know," Luca said. "But I'm not crazy about the idea of you and Angel in Rome right now."

"You're not the only one," Angel said. "But if McDermott is the only way to find out more about Murdock, and Murdock is the only way to call off Raneiro's dogs…"

Nico turned to her. "There's probably no point asking this, but…"

"No," Angel said. "I'm not staying here while you go. We're in this together, remember? Donati has a contract out on both of us, and on my brother, too. I'm not sitting here like some kind of princess while you do all the dirty work."

He sighed. "Do you have an address on McDermott?" he asked Luca.

Luca waved at the envelope. "It's all there, along with a list of his most frequented haunts."

"Great," Nico said. "Where are you going?"

"Meeting up with Elia and Marco in Miami," he said. "We'll lay low there for awhile, stay on the ready in case you need us."

Nico nodded, then slid from the booth as Luca did the same. Nico clasped his back as they embraced.

"I owe you."

"You don't owe me a thing," Luca said. "Call if you need us."

Angel gave him a hug. "Will you be okay?"

He laughed. "Don't worry about me. I'll be fine."

She looked up into his blue eyes. He'd become like a brother to her, and she felt a pang of fear at the thought of something happening to him. "Somebody has to do the worrying around here," she said.

He chuckled and kissed her cheek. Then he was gone.

# 17

Nico arranged a flat in Trastevere that night. It was easy to do online with one of the credit cards, and they found a flight out of Albany the next day. He disassembled and ditched his weapon in a dumpster and they left early the next morning. There were a few tense moments in Customs — it was obvious Angel was nervous about the fake documents — but then they were cleared and on their way to the gate.

He and Angel sat at the edge of the crowd while they waited for the plane to board. The security checkpoint should have given him comfort. It wasn't unheard of to smuggle a weapon into an airport with a few well placed bribes, but it was risky, and Nico didn't think it was a risk Raneiro would take.

Still, Nico knew better than anyone that a weapon wasn't required if you wanted to kill a man. He could kill a man ten different ways with his bare hands, and he had no doubt Raneiro's men were as effective. He sat next to Angel, maintaining an expression of boredom while scanning the crowd for anyone who might have been sent for them. He'd seemingly bought them some time with Raneiro, but Nico wasn't fool enough to actually trust him, and he didn't breath easy until they were on the plane, safely ensconced in first class. He wanted as few people as possible to remember them, and he still had plenty of money stashed in offshore accounts, a precaution passed along by his father. Their business was a dangerous one. It was impossible to know when politics or legalities might force one to flee.

And it was always better to be safe than sorry.

Once they were on the plane, he took advantage of the sparsely populated first class cabin to let down his guard. Rome would be risky. There was every possibility Raneiro had set him up, planted Desmond McDermott there to lure Nico to Raneiro's home turf. But somehow Nico didn't think so. The more he read about Murdock, the more it didn't sit right. He thought about what Luca had said.

*Drugs, trafficking, illegal weapons...*

Maybe he was off base. Maybe Sean Murdock was nothing more than a businessman with enough proprietary software development to take over the world. Enough power to make him a target for someone like Raneiro Donati. But Nico sensed urgency behind Raneiro's request, his forced apathy a careful disguise for raw anticipation.

No, Raneiro wanted the Darknet file, and he wanted Nico to get it for him. Nico was almost sure of it. And while he wasn't crazy about entering Reneiro's home turf with Angel, they didn't have a choice. The fastest way to Sean Murdock was through his childhood friend, Desmond McDermott.

They reached cruising altitude, and Angel stretched out next to him. He caught a glimpse of creamy skin as her dress hiked up to her thigh. His cock responded like a good soldier, and he shifted in his seat, watched her lips close around the glass in her hand. She wasn't trying to be sexy. She was just sitting there, hair pulled back into a loose ponytail, some of the pieces escaping around her face.

But goddamn. He wanted her.

It didn't matter that her naked body had been under his only hours before. He would never have enough of her, and his eyes traveled from her full mouth to the hollow at the base of her throat, then continued to the suggestive swell of her breasts under the simple black dress.

He shifted uncomfortably in his seat. Fuck. It was going to be a long ten hours to their layover in London.

His cock was still pulsing ten minutes later when she got up to go to the bathroom. He took a quick look down the aisle where the flight attendants were doing drink service and got up from his seat.

# 18

She was closing the bathroom door when she felt someone at her back. She turned to find Nico slipping in behind her.

"Nico, what are you - "

He shut the door and locked it, then silenced her with his lips. She had no choice but to open her mouth. Her body had a mind of its own when it came to him, and she was barely aware they were still on the plane as he turned her body in the minuscule lavatory and lifted her onto the tiny counter next to the sink.

Her arms snaked around his neck as he stroked her tongue with his. She opened her legs, her dress hiking up to her hips, and he moved in closer, the rigid length of his erection against her panties sending a rush of wetness to her core. He nibbled on her lower lip, then kissed his way to her ear, sank his teeth into her earlobe until she moaned, her head falling to the side. He responded by licking his way to her collarbone, using one hand to slip the dress off her shoulder until one side of her bra was visible.

The plane jerked as they hit a patch of turbulence, and she clutched the edge of the counter as Nico put a strong arm around her hips.

"I've got you," he murmured, pulling the lacy fabric of her bra down to expose her breast.

He cupped the mound of flesh in one hand and lowered his lips to the erect nipple. She gasped as the heat of his mouth closed around her cool skin. It was strangely erotic, the plane swaying around them as he tongued the little bud, the moisture between her legs soaking her underwear as his cock strained for her.

She reached under his shirt, let her fingers travel the tight ripple of his abs on their way to his belt buckle. Her pussy was throbbing in anticipation, the desire to clench down on him while he invaded her almost overwhelming.

He took her hand away from his belt buckle. "Not yet, baby."

"We have to hurry," she gasped as he lowered his body, wedging himself between her legs, the broad expanse of his shoulders almost spanning the width of the room.

"No, we don't," he said, pressing her legs open wider. "You'll come when you're ready to come. And when I'm ready for you to come."

A second later his mouth was on her, his tongue dragging through her slick folds while she arched her back, trying not to cry out from the ecstasy of it. He slid two fingers inside her while he latched onto her clit, moving in and out of her while the plane vibrated under her ass, the hum of it working in concert with Nico's movement to create a rhythm all its own. She looked down and felt more wetness pool between her legs at the sight of his dark head between there. She moved her hips against his mouth while she watched, the experience strangely erotic, voyeuristic, as if she were watching someone else while being pleasured at the same time.

He took his mouth off her clit and replaced it with his thumb, making circles while he looked up at her, his eyes hooded with desire. "You taste so good, baby."

She leaned back as far as the little room would allow and rotated her hips on his fingers as he lowered his mouth back to her sex, flicking his tongue against the swollen seed of her clit, lapping at it like he couldn't get enough while the orgasm built inside her. She caught a glimpse of them in the mirror: her spread legs, Nico's head between them, her breast straining over the fabric of her bra.

Everything else disappeared behind the hum of the plane and Nico's hot mouth on her pussy. She was delirious with need, the orgasm closing in, blackening the edges of her vision as she tumbled toward oblivion. Then he hooked his fingers inside her, putting pressure on the secret spot that gave her the final push into paradise. She let go of everything, let herself fall into the light of release as she shuddered around his fingers, the two of them in a world all their own.

She had her hands on his belt buckle the second he rose to his feet, her desire for him undimmed by the shattering orgasm he'd given her with his mouth. She wouldn't be complete until he was inside her, taking her the way only he could. She freed his cock — thick, heavy, hard — and opened her legs wider for him while he pulled a condom from his wallet. She stroked him while he opened it, palming his length and reveling in the way he grew bigger, harder, with every stroke, his need for her obvious, irrefutable.

He handed her the condom, and she rolled it onto his massive cock, then positioned the tip at her entrance. He dragged it through the wetness of her folds, slick with the juices from her orgasm, then over her clit.

"Now," she gasped. "Now, Nico."

"Now, baby?" He slapped her clit with his cock, and the torture of having him so close to filling her almost sent her over the edge. "You want it?"

"I want it," she said. "Please."

"Please." His chuckle was dark, laced with sex. "What a good girl you are."

He leaned in, covered her mouth with his and drove into her. She cried out in his mouth, the pleasure of his tongue working with the feel of him pulling out of her, sliding back in. He held her head between his hands, plundering her mouth while she pulled at his rock hard ass, trying to get him farther inside her, wishing there was room to bend over so he could fill her from behind.

He tugged at her hips until she was lifted off the counter, suspended over the floor, her legs wrapped around his thighs while he plunged into her faster, harder, his cock hitting the top of her while his body rubbed against her clit, the friction pushing her higher.

She felt his orgasm build with her own. Felt him thicken inside her as he moved faster. She was almost there, but she wanted him to jump with her, wanted to leap into the light with him by her side.

"I'm going to come," she said. "Come with me, baby."

The words finished him off, and he groaned, shuddering against her, still moving as she milked him for every lost drop.

She let her head fall forward onto his shoulder while they both caught their breath. The rest of the world had ceased to exist, and she was surprised when someone started banging on the door.

"Is everything all right in there?" a voice called from outside the lavatory.

"Everything's fine!" she called. "Be right out."

Nico started to laugh, and Angel clamped a hand over his mouth, her own body shaking as she tried to contain her laughter.

# 19

The flat Nico had rented was hidden in a tiny, cobblestone alley in
Trastevere behind a facade of mustard yellow stucco. Nico retrieved
the key from the owner of the ground floor unit, and after a few
words with her in Italian, they trudged up a flight of narrow stairs to
the one bedroom apartment.

As soon as Nico opened the door, Angel wished they'd come
under different circumstances. The place was small but gorgeous,
with expansive windows rising to a tall, polished wood ceiling.
There was an efficient kitchen that opened onto a living room with a
fireplace. The bedroom was cozy, and the bathroom was dominated
by an enormous claw-foot tub with old brass fittings. It was a place
that begged for lazy Sunday mornings with espresso and panettone,
for cozy nights and long conversations by the fire with a bottle of
wine.

"It's nice," Nico said after they walked through the rooms.

"It's perfect," she said.

He wrapped his arms around her and pulled her close. "You're
awfully easy to please."

"I have you," she said. "That's all I need."

She pushed away the dread that dropped over her as she said it.
It felt a little like tempting the fates, and she reminded herself not to

take anything for granted. Not to assume either of them would make it out of this alive. They had now. It would have to be enough.

"Let's get some breakfast and do a little recon," Nico said.

She fluttered her eyelashes dramatically. "Why, you sweet talker, you."

He laughed and swatted her on the ass as she turned away.

They stopped at a little cafe and staked claim to a table on the street. Angel spent the next hour people watching and dunking her buttery cornetto into the best cappuccino she'd ever tasted while Nico studied a map of the city. Finally, he lowered the map.

And damn, he was beautiful.

In sunglasses, tailored slacks, and a perfectly fitted white button down open at the neck, he looked as at home in Rome as any of the stylish men passing by on the street. She thought about his mouth on her on the plane, the reflection in the mirror of his body joining hers as he fucked her, and was wet for him all over again.

A slow smile spread to his lips. "You look like that cat that ate the canary," he said.

She took a sip of her cappuccino. "Something like that."

"I want to know more about that look in your eyes later," he said. "But first, we need to rent a car."

They rented a small red convertible and headed out of Rome. The air was warm and dry as they continued into the verdant, leafy hills of Lazio, the brine of the sea mixing with the smell of oranges and the musky scent of bay trees. It was hard not to be in the moment, and little by little, Angel's apprehension faded into the background. The future was still uncertain, but wasn't it always? All anyone has is now.

After about an hour, Nico pulled off the main road and continued up a series of smaller, windy streets. Finally, he turned off the road and brought the car to a stop near some bushes by the side of the road.

"We'll walk from here," he said.

They got out of the car, and Angel followed him down the road and to the right. They came up short just before the start of an iron fence.

"This is McDermott's villa," Nico said. "We need to get a handle on the security before we decide how to approach him."

"How are we going to do that out here?" she asked, looking up at the pointed spires of the fence.

"Very carefully," he said. "We need to make sure we're not spotted, so keep an eye out for cameras."

They started by walking along the side of the property, following the fence through orange and olive trees, being careful to stay far enough away that the cameras — and there were cameras she saw now, spaced about fifty feet apart — wouldn't pick them up.

The back of the property abutted a rocky cliff. That was a no go as far as access.

They backtracked to the front of the property and crossed the street, then walked the other side of the fence, just to be sure it was set up the same way. It was, and they headed back to the front gate.

"What now?" she asked.

"Let's hang around," he said. "See if anyone comes in through the gate so we can determine the entrance protocol. It's a long shot, but we're here; we might as well cover our bases before resorting to Plan B."

"What's Plan B?"

"Find him at the local bar when he goes for his nightly pint according to the schedule Luca gave us," Nico said.

"Not very private," Angel said.

"Exactly."

They used the trees at the side of the road to hide their position. It was another hour before they heard the sound of gravel crunching under tires in the distance. Angel nudged Nico, sitting next to her on the ground.

"Someone's coming."

They got up and watched as a sleek, black sports car pulled up to the gate. A hand emerged from the driver's side window to push a button on the control panel. A few seconds later a voice came over the intercom and spoke in Italian. The driver answered — also in Italian — and an electronic buzz was followed by the hum of the gates swinging open.

Angel looked at Nico. "Want to make a run for it after the car?"

He shook his head. "The driver said he had a message from Sean. This doesn't feel good to me."

"What do you mean?"

"I don't know," Nico said. "My gut tells me it's a bad idea to get caught behind those gates."

"You think it's a trap?" Angel asked. "That Raneiro could be counting on us coming here?"

"I don't know. I'd just feel better if we stayed out in the open where we can get away if we need to. This place is pretty locked down. We have no idea who's inside, and once we're in, getting out might be just as difficult."

"So we catch McDermott at the bar then," Angel said.

"And hope he's alone," Nico added.

They headed into town, checked out the pub where Desmond McDermott was reported to take his pint, and spent the rest of the afternoon exploring the village. It was intimate and quaint, nestled in the hills outside Rome. They traversed the cobblestone streets and looked in the shops, then took a break for an early dinner at a cozy trattoria. By the time the sun went down, Angel had almost forgotten why they were there. It had been a pleasant few hours with Nico, one of the rare moments when they were allowed to be simply a man and woman in love. She wondered if they would get the chance to have more moments like it, if there would ever come a time when they wouldn't be fighting for their lives or the lives of someone they loved.

Just before nine, they ordered a couple of pints and took a seat in a booth at the rear of the pub. Angel sat with her back to the door. Nico sat across from her where he could see everyone who came and went. Beyond their table, a narrow hall exited onto an alley that would give them access to the main road if they needed to make a quick getaway. The information Luca gave them indicated that McDermott usually went for his pint alone, but they wouldn't take it for granted; they would watch to make sure he was unaccompanied before approaching him. Still, an alternate exit was a good back up plan in case anything went wrong.

Angel's eyelids were feeling heavy, jet lag finally catching up with her, when the bell on the door to the pub jingled. Nico's eyes lit with recognition.

"Is it him?" Angel asked, not wanting to draw attention to herself by turning around.

Nico nodded.

"Is he alone?"

"So far," Nico said. "Let's give it a minute."

Nico nursed his beer, his expression bored. Angel wasn't fooled. She'd come to recognize the attentive light in his eye. It told her that nothing was beyond his notice. Every movement, every person, every detail, was being recorded in his mind, filed away for future use. It made her feel safe, but also sad. He deserved more than to be watchful all the time, than to be worried for his life and the lives of the people around him. But would he be happy in another kind of life?

She still didn't know the answer.

"I don't suppose I can talk you into staying here while I talk to him?" Nico finally asked her.

She shook her head. "In for a penny, in for a pound."

He nodded. "Stay close. And if there's trouble, follow my lead."

# 20

Desmond McDermott looked like he was alone, but Nico knew that was no guarantee. Not for the first time, he wished he had a weapon. He could have secured one on the black market in Rome, but they needed to stay under Raneiro's radar, and since they didn't know how long they'd be here, it hadn't seemed like a worthwhile risk. If Nico had his way, they'd get a lead on Sean Murdock from McDermott and be out of Rome by morning. The more distance between them and Raneiro the better.

He set his nearly empty pint on the bar and slid onto the stool next to Desmond McDermott. Angel sat on the other side of him, and he instinctively angled his body to cover hers as much as possible. Desmond McDermott looked harmless enough — blond hair, ruddy complexion, average height with a belly going soft — but Nico wouldn't bet Angel's safety on it.

"Buona sera," Nico said, when Desmond's gaze cut his way.

Desmond nodded. "Buona sera."

Nico waved at the bartender for a refill, watching as he filled another glass and set it down on the bar. "Grazie."

He took a drink of the beer, biding his time. When the bartender moved toward the other end of the bar, Nico spoke without looking at the man next to him.

"How is Sean these days?"

He saw McDermott turn to look at him in his peripheral vision. "Who are you?"

"Not important," Nico said.

"The hell you say," McDermott said his Irish brogue getting thicker with his agitation.

"Word is you and Murdock have had a falling out," Nico said. "And I think you and I might be on the same side."

The statement was risky, based purely on speculation drawn from all that he'd read about McDermott and Murdock. Luca had been right; according to every available source, they had been like brothers. There were very few things that could destroy that kind of friendship, and while Nico couldn't be sure, he was betting it had something to do with Sean's rumored illegal activity.

McDermott moved to stand, and Nico clamped a hand firmly but quietly on his wrist. Angel shifted in her seat.

"Please, sit." McDermott hesitated, and Nico took advantage of the opportunity to expand on his message. "I mean you no harm."

McDermott settled back in his seat. "What do you want?"

"Sean has something in his possession," Nico said. "Something dangerous. I simply want to insure its safekeeping."

He almost held his breath on the bluff. He had no idea what was on the Darknet file. but if it was important to Raneiro — and it was — it had to be something that could be leveraged for greater power. It was the only thing worth more than making an example out of Nico to everyone in the Syndicate. And if it could be used to make Raneiro more powerful, it was dangerous, plain and simple. That Nico wanted to insure its safekeeping remained to be seen, but he'd say what he had to in order to secure Angel's safety.

"I don't know anything about that," McDermott said a little too vehemently.

Nico took a drink of his beer. "I don't believe that."

"Sean and I are on the outs, like you said."

"I'm not looking for anything specific." Nico lowered his voice. "Just point me in the right direction."

"And why would I do that?" McDermott said. "I don't know you."

Nico nodded, meeting his eyes. "Someone's coming for what Murdock has. And if you don't want it to fall into the wrong hands, I promise that you want it to be me."

McDermott turned his attention back to his beer. "Sean has a lot of things people want," he said softly.

"I'm not talking about software," Nico said. "But I think you know that."

McDermott gave him a sidelong glance, then stood. "You best be on your way before you get yourself into trouble," he said, a little too loudly.

Nico was puzzled by his change in demeanor until he threw some cash down on the bar and spoke under his breath.

"Everything that matters to Sean is in Dublin."

It was little more than a whisper, but Nico heard it loud and clear. He watched McDermott exit the bar and then glanced around before looking at Angel. "We need to get out of here."

He was relieved when she didn't say anything. She just stood and let him usher her out the back door to the alley. He felt his lack of weapon as they made their way through the darkened streets back to the car.

"What's wrong?" Angel finally asked as he navigated out of the village.

"Nothing probably," he said.

"Probably?"

"I got the feeling Sean was being watched," he said. "I was worried we were made."

"Do you think it was a trap by Raneiro?" Angel asked.

"I don't know," Nico said. "But I'll feel better when we get out of here."

They dropped the car off at the rental office and walked back to the flat, Angel leaning drowsily on his arm. By the time he put the key in the door, he was starting to believe he was just being paranoid. Raneiro had to know Nico would contact Desmond McDermott. It was the easiest way to gain private information about Sean Murdock. Raneiro could have had people waiting outside McDermott's villa. He could have had someone tail McDermott and kill Nico and Angel as soon as they made contact. By giving Nico so specific a task, Raneiro had made him an easy target. No, if Raneiro Donati wanted him dead, he'd be dead by now.

He almost believed the internal argument until he opened the door and heard the click of the gun.

# 21

Her eyes barely had time to adjust to the light in the living room before she spotted the men. There were two of them; one tall and thin and standing by the windows, the other big and beefy, his neck the size of a tree trunk, sitting in the chair by the room's writing desk.

Both of them had guns.

"Looks like our friends have had a nice day sightseeing," Skinny said, his voice laced with a thick Italian accent.

Beefy sighed. "Young love. Ain't it grand?"

"It sure is," Skinny said. He waved the gun at them. "Come in and shut the door. And don't get any big ideas about running. We're not alone."

Angel cut a glance at Nico, saw the internal battle being waged in his mind. A moment later he shut the door and stepped into the room, angling his body in front of hers in a familiar gesture of protection.

"Come in, come in," Beefy said. "We're just going to have a little chat."

She stepped into the room, taking advantage of her position behind Nico to scan the room for something they might use as a weapon. It didn't take long to realize it was futile unless she wanted to go slapstick and hit one of them over the head with a lamp. Somehow she didn't think it would be very effective agains the cold-eyed, dead-voiced men in their room. Had this been Raneiro's plan all along? Get them out of the US — away from Luca and anyone else who might help them — and kill them here on his home turf?

"What do you want?" Nico asked.

"Just wondering what brings you to our fair city," Skinny said. "Somehow you don't strike me as tourists."

"Who sent you?" Nico asked.

Skinny stood, cocking the gun. "I think you're confused. We ask the questions here."

Nico nodded, taking another step in front of Angel. "I'm on an errand for Raneiro," he said. "Just following his instructions."

"Who the fuck is Raneiro?" Beefy looked confused.

Nico's confidence seemed to falter, but he didn't have time to say anything else before Beefy stalked toward him. Angel instinctively stepped forward as he raised his hand to strike Nico with the gun.

But Nico was way ahead of him. His hand shot up, blocking Beefy's arm as one leg came up to kick the weapon from his hand. It clattered to the floor just as Skinny came up behind her. She'd been too busy watching Nico to see the gunman edge his way toward her, and she heard the click of the gun at her temple over the sound of the bones crunching in Beefy's arms as Nico twisted it behind him. He pointed the gun pointed at the back of the man's head.

"Unless you care less about this bitch than I care about my partner, I'd suggest you drop the gun," Skinny said.

Nico looked up, caught sight of Angel with the gun to her head, and dropped the weapon.

Beefy straightened, massaging his arm, and took the gun back from Nico, then cracked it hard across Nico's face. A cut opened up over his eye, and blood streamed down his cheek.

"Now that wasn't polite," Skinny said. "We were just having a conversation."

"Didn't look like that was the direction things were going," Nico said, blotting at the gash on his forehead with the hem of his T-shirt.

"Please let me kill this son-of-a-bitch," Beefy said, pointing the gun at Nico.

"Sean wouldn't like it," Skinny said.

Sean? The men were sent by Sean Murdock, software engineer extraordinaire?

"Fuck," Beefy muttered.

"Just tell us why you were talking to McDermott," Skinny said to Nico.

"Raneiro Donati wanted to offer him a job," Nico said.

The last name triggered a flicker of recognition on the faces of Skinny and Beefy. Sean Murdock might own Dublin, but Rome belonged to Raneiro Donati.

She tried to keep her face impassive. Would Sean Murdock check their story? Would it cause trouble for Raneiro? Negate the deal they had with him? She didn't know, but it's not like they had a choice. It was as good a story as any she could have come up with.

Skinny looked confused. "What kind of job?"

"Fuck if I know," Nico said. "I'm just the errand boy. Donati heard McDermott was out of a job with Murdock. Asked me to feel him out. Maybe he's looking for some brains to add to his brawn."

"What did McDermott say?" Beefy asked.

"Said he was still under contract with Sean Murdock," Nico answered.

"That's it?" Beefy asked.

"That's it," Nico said.

They lowered their weapons. "Then I suggest you get out of town," Beefy said. "Sean doesn't like anyone sniffing around his people. Makes him nervous."

Nico nodded. "On our way out first thing tomorrow morning."

"Good. Tell Donati to find his own talent."

Nico nodded as they shoved past him to the door.

# 22

They took the first flight to London the next morning. Angel had slept fitfully, half listening for any strange sound. Nico didn't seem to do any better; every time she looked at him, his eyes were open, his posture making it clear that he was on alert. They were exhausted by the time they reached the apartment they'd rented in London, and they collapsed into bed with hardly a word.

They woke nearly twenty four hours later, the weak London sun spilling gray light into the one-bedroom flat. They threw on clothes and stopped for breakfast on their way to the market where they bought food for the apartment. Angel had no idea how long they'd be in London — Nico said it depended on how things went with Farrell Black — but they were well supplied for a few days at least.

When they got back to the apartment, Nico pulled out two new Tracphones. He kept one for himself and handed one to Angel.

"Call David while you can."

"What are you doing with that one?" she asked, looking at the phone in his hand.

"Calling Luca," he said. "I don't want to approach Farrell Black without him."

"Are you sure we can trust Farrell?" she asked.

He seemed to think about it. "No one can trust Farrell. He's only loyal to his own cause. It's not ideal, but it makes him a better bet than the soldiers who are willing to die for Raneiro."

"I'm still not clear how Farrell can help us," Angel said. "It's our job to get the Darknet file for Raneiro. Won't he be pissed if we enlist Farrell's help?"

"We're not enlisting Farrell's help with the file."

"We're not?"

He shook his head. "We need supplies — weapons, surveillance and communications equipment, transportation. It will take too long to put it together myself, and Farrell will have a better idea how to get it all in place in Dublin."

"So we're asking him for logistical support?"

"Farrell doesn't do anything for free," he said. "We're hiring him for logistical support. Assuming he wants to be hired."

She thought about the massive man she'd met the last time they'd been in London, when she was still trying to figure out the truth about her father. The air around Farrell Black had been charged with danger, like the atmosphere before an electrical storm. Until then, she'd thought Nico was the most dangerous man she'd ever met. Being around Farrell showed her there were levels to violence that she couldn't yet fathom and was in no hurry to discover. She didn't love the idea of telling him their plans, but they weren't exactly overflowing with possibilities.

Nico went into the bedroom to call Luca, and Angel dialed the house in Maine. It rang twice before Sara picked up. Angel caught the tail end of her laughter before she spoke.

"Hello?"

"Sara, it's Angel."

"Angel!" She could almost see Sara's smile. "How are you? Is everything okay?"

"Everything's fine," she said into the phone. "I just wanted to check in, see how you and David are getting along."

"Well, he's kicking my ass in chess," she said. "But other than that, we're doing great."

"She beat me in checkers," David shouted in the background.

Sara laughed. "A dubious honor."

Angel smiled. Hearing David's voice made her aware of the ocean between them, and she suddenly missed him like crazy.

"Is he taking his meds?" she asked.

"Hold on," Sara said. She heard Sara's footsteps and knew she was moving to another room where she could speak freely. "He's doing really well, Angel. Really well. Taking his meds. Eating. Sleeping. Even talking some about what happened."

"Really?" Angel said. "What about it?"

"Nothing specific," Sara said. "Just… you know, working through it. I think it's good for him to be here."

Angel leaned her head against the glass door leading onto the balcony. *And good to be away from me probably,* she thought.

She tried not to feel bitter. It was bound to be harder for David to talk to her about everything that had happened. She had been so deeply entrenched in the Syndicate's Boston operation, in seeking revenge for what had happened to Nico and David. Maybe David just need to talk to someone who didn't have all that baggage.

"I'm glad you're there for him, Sara," she said. "Thank you."

She meant it. David was the most important person in the world to her. She needed him to be okay. However that happened was all right with her.

"It's my pleasure," she said. "You want to talk to him?"

"Please."

"Hold on." She heard a shuffling sound on the other end of the phone, and a moment later David's voice came over the receiver.

"Hey, sis."

"Hey, loser."

He laughed. "Where are you?"

"I could tell you, but then I'd have to kill you," she said.

"Got it. But you're okay?"

"I'm okay," she said. "I just miss you."

"I miss you, too," he said. "But don't worry. I'm fine."

"Really?"

"Really," he said. "Sara's really great. I'm taking care of myself, figuring some things out."

"Yeah?" she asked.

"Yeah."

"Good. You guys have everything you need?"

"Ed brought fresh supplies last night ahead of schedule," he said. "We're all set."

"I'm glad." She turned as Nico came back into the room. "Well, I better go. It's nice to hear your voice."

"You too, Ange. I love you."

"Love you, too. I'll call as soon as I can."

She hung up, took a deep breath against the sudden loss in her chest. Nico crossed the room and pulled her into his arms, like he sensed her melancholy.

"They okay?" he asked.

"They're good."

"You okay?"

She looked up at him and tried to smile. "I'm good."

He touched a finger to her temple, traced it down her cheek to her lips, then lowered his mouth to kiss her gently. It stole her breath, and she felt the tug between her legs that was her body's call to him. It didn't matter what was happening — she always wanted him. Always needed him.

He pulled away, ran his thumb along her lower lip, smiled. "Luca can't be here for a couple of days."

"What will we do until then?" she asked, looking up at him.

He grinned. "We'll think of something."

# 23

"I got Sean's compound on Google maps," Angel said.

Nico came back into the room and set two cups of coffee on the nightstand. Angel was sitting on the bed, dressed in one of his shirts with only a couple buttons done, her delicious body visible between the folds of crisp cotton, lithe legs stretched out in front of her. He slid behind her so they could both see the iPad while she rested against his chest. Her almost bare ass brushed against his cock. He was hard less than five seconds later.

She squirmed, twisting to look at him with a devilish grin. "Already?"

He grabbed her hips, pulled her back against him so he was nestled between the cheeks of her ass. "Always."

"Work first, play later," she said.

And it's not like they hadn't played. He'd fucked her senseless in the twenty-four hours they'd been in London. Now that the initial danger had passed, he couldn't get enough of her. He'd wanted to embed himself on her skin, brand her with his touch, make her his so completely that nothing would ever separate them again. He'd done all that and more, licking and driving and tasting and kissing and thrusting until there wasn't an inch of her he hadn't occupied. And still, it wasn't enough. He was finally starting to accept that it would never be enough.

"Too bad we can't see what kind of security he has there," Nico said, peering at the aerial image on the screen. Trying to focus on their mission with Angel between his legs was no easy task.

She tabbed over to another web page. "I did find this article on the house in Architectural Digest," Angel said. "It mentions a study. The journalist called it 'Murdock's private lair'."

"That sounds promising."

"Let's hope so," Angel said. "The house is twenty-five thousand square feet. It's going to take a long time to find every computer if it's not in his study."

"Did the article say anything about security?" he asked.

"No, but that's not unusual. AD is a high-end style magazine. Can Luca find out about security?" she asked.

"Doubtful," Nico said.

"So how will we know what we're up against when we try to get in?"

"I don't know." It pained him to admit it, but it was true. He didn't have enough information to plan their infiltration of Sean's compound. Not yet anyway. They were flying blind. It wasn't how he liked to work, but the old rules didn't apply. Now they had to be flexible, use the resources they had, even when it didn't seem like enough. "We'll get what we can from Farrell, head to Dublin, find a way in."

"Are we even sure the file is there?" she asked.

"No, but McDermott said anything that's important to Sean will be in Dublin. It's all we've got."

"How long until Luca gets here?" Angel asked.

"Sometime tomorrow," Nico said.

"What do you want to do until then?"

He took the tablet from her hand and set it on the nightstand, then pulled her onto his lap.

"You mean keeping you my prisoner in bed isn't an option?" he asked, nuzzling her neck until she giggled.

"We've been in bed a whole day already," she said. "I think we could both use some fresh air."

He didn't want fresh air. He just wanted her in his bed, her body moving under his while he made her come. But he saw her point.

"Fine," he said, hoisting her off his lap. "I'll feed you and show you the town, and after, you let me ravish you all I want."

She leaned back on her arms, rocked her knees open so he got the quickest glimpse of the paradise between her thighs. "After?"

He growled and pounced on the bed while she shrieked.

Two hours later they were showered and changed and on the streets of London. They started with crisp fish and chips and then took a double decker bus for a tour around the city. They'd both been to London — even before their ill-fated trip last fall — but everything felt different with Angel. He wanted to retrace his steps through life, do everything over again with her by his side. It was the height of luxury in their current circumstances: being silly, pretending they were like any other couple when the clock was ticking on their time together like it had been since the moment they met. He savored every smile, every touch of her hand, tried to memorize the shine in her eyes that she seemed to reserve just for him. Then he tried to tamp down the fear that rose in him at the thought of something happening to her. The fact that Raneiro wanted something from Sean Murdock meant that Murdock wasn't just a businessman, something made even more obvious by the thugs who'd accosted them in their room in Rome. It would be dangerous, and if he thought he stood a chance in hell at convincing Angel to stay behind, he'd try.

He glanced at her as she walked next to him. She looked so young, so vulnerable with her long hair swept into a ponytail. He would do anything to protect her, but he also knew she wasn't the same girl he'd kidnapped last year. For better or worse, she was stronger now, tougher. Maybe even too tough for her own good. And he'd recognized the light in her eyes when she'd talked about revenge. It was a light that had stared back at him from the mirror in the years following his parent's murder, a light that wasn't easily extinguished.

He would have to deal with that, reconcile it against their goal of getting out alive.

But this was precious time that they wouldn't have again. Once Luca arrived, they would have to talk to Farrell Black and move onto Dublin, plan their breach of Sean Murdock's computer.

Until then, she was his, and he wanted to savor every second with her. Wanted to give her as much happiness as he could.

He pulled her toward the river. "Come on."

She laughed. "Where are we going?"

"You'll see."

## 24

She let him pull her along. She enjoyed this happier, freer version of him, but it made her sad that she'd seen so little of it. He'd spent the two years after his parent's murder focused on getting justice for them, and the year since he'd gotten it had been filled with worry about the family, about her, about Raneiro's growing displeasure with the East Coast operation. She wondered how long it had been since he'd truly been free.

She stopped in her tracks when they reached the terminal for the London Eye, the gigantic ferris wheel looming above them over the Thames.

"Oh, no," she said, backing up. "No way."

"Come on," he said, recapturing her hand. "People go up in it every day. It's perfectly safe, and there's no better view of London."

He grinned under his sunglasses, and she knew she was doomed. She couldn't resist him.

They bought tickets and waited in a short line to board. It was mid-week, and they reached the front of the line in less than ten minutes. She expected to be ushered into one of the enclosed capsules with a bunch of other people — that's how it had been done it so far — but Nico gave the attendant a folded wad of cash, and he closed the door behind them, leaving them alone in a spacious pod surrounded by glass. A surfboard-shaped bench anchored the middle of the capsule, leaving the windows clear for anyone who wanted to stand.

She expected to lurch and sway as they rose into the air, but the motion was strangely smooth. She held onto a railing on the inside, and when she finally dared a look through the glass at the contraption, she saw that each capsule was welded into place so that only the wheel moved as it rotated, creating minimal movement in the pods.

They rose a little at a time, stopping every now and then as a fresh batch of passengers was loaded into the capsules below them. After a few minutes, she sat next to Nico on the bench, London spread out below them. There was Big Ben, Parliament, the many bridges over the Thames. It was all glorious and sparkling from up so high, the blue sky dotted with clouds that seemed to part for them as they moved higher.

"Gorgeous," she breathed.

"Yes."

His breath was close to her ear, and when she turned her head, his mouth touched her cheek. She closed her eyes, the feel of his lips causing goosebumps to rise on her skin. He wrapped her ponytail in his hand and tugged her head back. She gasped as he touched his tongue to her collarbone, the fabric of her skirt sliding upward as he moved his hand from her calf to her thigh, his touch electric against her skin.

She slipped a hand up his shirt, running her fingers along the swell of muscle on his back as he kissed his way up her throat. She was already wet, her panties sticking to her sex as his hand massaged her inner thigh, so close and not nearly close enough. She wiggled, sliding down a little, wanting his fingers inside her as he nipped at her earlobe. It didn't matter that he'd fucked her countless times in the past twenty-four hours. She wanted him again. She always wanted him.

His chuckle was low and smooth. "Easy now."

He kissed his way across her cheek, licking the corners of her lips. Her mouth parted of its own accord, ready and waiting for his tongue. He tugged at her lower lip with his teeth, and her core tightened between her legs as his hand moved farther up her thigh. He cupped the apex of her desire, teasing her pussy through the thin satin of her panties.

She turned her head a little, capturing his mouth with her lips, unable to wait. He gave a tug on the ponytail, reminding her who was in charge, and she whimpered as his tongue invaded her mouth at the same time. She arched her back, willing his other hand under the fabric of her underwear, her core aching for his fingers.

"You're soaked for me," he said against her mouth, moving his thumb over her clit through her underwear.

"Please," she begged.

"Please what?" he asked.

"I want your fingers inside me." She spread her legs a little more, oblivious to whether any of the passengers in the other capsules could see them.

He inched his hand to the edge of her underwear as he lowered his mouth to her breast, nipping at one of her erect nipples through the thin fabric of her T-shirt. She moved her hand to the front of his pants, rubbed against the swell of his cock, straining to be free. But when she started to work his belt buckle, he stilled her hand.

"Not this time, baby."

"Why?"

He pushed aside her panties and slid his fingers into her. She gasped.

"Don't ask questions," he said. "Just relax."

She leaned back on her arms, the height dizzying as Nico penetrated her while making slow circles around her clit with the fleshy pad of his thumb. She moved her hips to his rhythm while he thrust his fingers in and out of her, moisture surging between her legs, her clit swelling as the climax started rumbling in her bones.

He kissed his way up her neck. "You're going to come for me, aren't you, baby?" he murmured against her skin.

"Yes," she gasped.

"I love to watch you come," he said. "Have I ever told you that?"

His words aroused her further, and her sex tightened around his fingers. "No."

"I do," he said, kissing the corners of her mouth. "Watching you come makes me hard, makes me want to fuck you until you scream."

It was like pouring gasoline on a smoldering wildfire. She could almost feel him sinking inside her wet heat, filling her up until he poured into her. She moaned, moving her hips faster against his hand, letting the friction of his thumb on her clit build while he fucked her with his fingers. She opened her eyes and the sky spun, the world tilting as the orgasm closed in on her.

They were descending now, working their way back toward the river a little at a time, the bottom falling out of her stomach while she raced closer and closer toward her climax. The sensation was dizzying — climbing and falling and surging while Nico's fingers moved inside her, his tongue pillaging her mouth, his words forcing forbidden images into her mind.

"Do it, baby," he murmured in her ear. "I want to feel that beautiful pussy come on my fingers."

It sent her over the edge, pushing her off the cliff all at once until light exploded behind her eyes. She shook against him, his fingers still moving, his thumb still working her clit, until she came again, the second orgasm piling on top of the first until her whole body trembled with the force of it.

When it was over, she lay there, watching the big ferris wheel move around them as she slowly came back to reality. A minute later, Nico leaned down, kissed her full on the mouth, and straightened her skirt. Then he whispered in her ear.

"I estimate you have less than two minutes to gather your thoughts before that door opens."

She sat up as they stopped just above the loading platform. She laughed, punching him playfully in the arm. "Thanks a lot."

# 25

Luca arrived two days later looking as calm as ever. He didn't say anything about where he'd been or how he'd gotten to London, but he and Nico immediately went to work talking about Farrell Black and the help they hoped to gain from him. Angel listened, trying to avoid the feeling of doom that seeped into her lungs at the talk of weapons and additional man power. It was all too familiar. Too much like London. Like LA.

Finally, Nico excused himself to take care of business ahead of the meeting with Farrell later that night. Angel needed a dress for Farrell's club, so Luca agreed to accompany her to Bond Street.

"You're not going to give me the slip, are you?" he asked as they stepped into a taxi.

She laughed. "Not this time."

He settled back in the seat. "Glad to hear it. I'm not sure my ego would survive."

They hit up Selfridges and Vuitton before she settled on a gorgeous slip of a dress at Dolce and Gabbana. The conservative black lace top gave way to a jewel encrusted red skirt that was short enough to be almost scandalous. She picked up a pair of tall black boots with four inch heels at Burberry and called it a day. They stopped for lunch on the way back to the flat, and Angel studied

Luca across the table, wondering what was going on behind those blue eyes.

"How have you been?" she asked as she tucked into her food.

He looked suspiciously at her over his shepherds pie. "Fine."

She put down her fork and leveled her eyes at him.

"What?"

"I consider us friends," she said. "Do you?"

He shrugged. "Sure."

Why did she have the feeling Luca didn't really consider anybody but Nico a friend?

"I'm trying to have a conversation with you here," she said. "What went down in Boston was messy, and that's not even counting the shit show in LA. You've been excised from the New York family - "

"Not my family anymore," he interrupted.

He meant because of Nico, and she was struck all over again by his unyielding loyalty to the man she loved. "I understand, but it's still a loss, isn't it? You once told me the Vitale family was your family. How are you doing without that?"

She wasn't trying to pry. She just wanted him to know that she was friend. That he could talk if he wanted to do do.

"Nico is the Vitale family," Luca said. "He's my brother. I go where he goes."

She took another bite and studied him across the table. "I guess I just wonder if you get lonely."

"I don't," he said without hesitation.

"Sara - "

He put his fork down. "Look, I appreciate your concern, Angel. But I'm fine. I've been on my own for a long time. It's best for me that way. Sara's nice, but I'm not cut out for something long term."

"Why?" she asked.

"Why?"

"Yeah," she said. "Everybody needs somebody."

"Not me," he said. "Now can we please leave this alone? I always thought it would be nice to have a sister, but I didn't expect her to be so nosy."

She laughed. "Fine. Just… you know, I'm here if you ever want to talk."

"Noted."

"And I hope you won't close your heart to the idea of loving someone someday."

"Also noted," he said through clenched teeth.

Nico was waiting when they got back to the apartment. He didn't say anything about where he'd been or what he'd been doing, and Angel knew better than to ask. He'd tell her when he was ready. She took a nap while he and Luca strategized their meeting with Farrell.

It was after ten when she started getting ready to go to the club. The dress's skirt was showy, so she opted for smokey eye makeup and nude lips. She dried her hair until it was straight and silky and was zipping up the boots when Nico walked into the bedroom to get dressed.

"Me-ow," he said when she stood.

She smiled. "I'll take that as a compliment."

He crossed the room, his eyes liquid with lust. Sliding his arms around her waist, he cupped her ass, bare under the black thong she'd chosen to go with the dress. The space between her legs turned molten as he pressed her against him, his cock already hard for her.

"How am I supposed to concentrate on Farrell Black when you look like that?" he asked, his voice husky.

She reached up, wrapped her arms around his neck and tipped her head back to look at him. "I'm sure you'll manage."

"Don't be so sure." He kissed the corner of her mouth so slowly, so seductively, that she felt her panties turn damp. He squeezed her ass. "I'll be too busy thinking about this." He slid a hand around to the front of her dress and thumbed her clit over her underwear. "And this."

"If you don't stop it, that's all I'll be thinking about too." She stepped away, straightened her dress. "And that can't be good for business."

He was still laughing when she left the room.

They called a cab and made their way to Farrell's club. She was pretty sure she was surrounded by the two best looking men in London, and if the circumstances had been different, she would have felt like the luckiest woman alive. Nico was in a charcoal gray suit over a sweater of the finest cashmere, his sharp features standing in sharp relief under the dark hair combed back from his forehead. Luca was no less handsome in a black suit and metallic gray button down that would have looked cheesy on anyone but him. It brought out the blue in his eyes, and Angel couldn't help feeling a little hedonistic with two such gorgeous men flanking her.

They made their way to the outskirts of town and stopped outside a rundown building with no markings. Two men flanked a big metal door, their expressions bored, eyes blank. They stepped aside, and she couldn't help wondering what would have happened if she'd come here alone. Had she been considered part of the inner circle by virtue of her position in Boston? Did the men who worked for Farrell Black know the faces of every Boss in the Syndicate? Or did this kind of access require membership of a different sort?

Nico led the way into a small vestibule lined with purple lights. Luca remained close behind her as they made their way down a flight of narrow stairs. Techno drifted from the club below, growing louder as they neared the basement. They emerged into the warehouse-like space of Farrell's club. It was industrial — concrete floors, exposed pipes, brick walls — made lush by the writhing bodies dancing in the middle of the cavernous room. At the front, Vito Corleone played in the garden with his grandson on a giant movie screen, the sound muted. The light-hearted movements of the actors seemed strangely foreboding against the backdrop of the music.

A bald man with a headset greeted them with a nod and tipped his head at the stairs at the back of the room. Angel thought she remembered him from the last time she'd been here. It seemed like a lifetime ago.

Nico reached back for her hand. She took it and followed him up the stairs, past several muscled men who watched them with careful eyes. They continued to the end of a utilitarian hallway and a closed door on the left. Two men who could have been clones of the others guarded the door, their legs spread, arms crossed in front of them, semiautomatic weapons holstered at their sides. Danger hung in the air like smoke.

"He's expecting you," one of them said, moving aside for them to enter.

Angel didn't know if it was because Nico had told Farrell they were coming or if word had spread from the guards at the front of the club, but a moment later, she was inside the room with Nico. It was only when she looked back that she realized Luca wasn't there. Had they stopped him from entering as some kind of precaution against Farrell being outgunned? The possibility sent a trickle of ice water through her veins.

She turned back to look at the man they'd come to meet and had to force herself not to edge toward the door. Every instinct in her body screamed at her to get away from him. It wasn't just the sheer size of him — at least a couple of inches taller than Nico's already impressive height. It was something raw and cold that seemed to surround him like a layer of age-old ice.

Angel had gotten used to being around fearsome men. Despite Nico's love for her, she didn't delude herself into thinking he was anything but what he was: a criminal, and a violent one when the situation called for it. But where there had always been humanity in Nico's eyes — violence, yes, but also humanity — Farrell Black's eyes were as still and empty as a glacial lake.

Tattoos snaked up his chest from the dark blue shirt that barely seemed able to contain him, and the scar above his eye seemed more deeply etched than it had been a year ago. He regarded them with calm interest, his arms crossed in front of his chest. The silence stretched thin in the room.

Finally, he spoke, his eyes settling on Angel. "Well Vitale, what kind of cluster-fuck has this girl gotten you into now?"

## 26

"Leave her out of it," Nico said, forcing his voice calm.

Farrell sat down with a smirk. What a dick. "You're the one who brought her."

"I protect what's mine," Nico said. "I think you know a little something about that."

A shadow crossed Farrell's normally placid features. It was all Nico needed to say.

"I thought you were dead," Farrell said, clipping the end off a cigar.

"Reports of my death have been greatly exaggerated," Nico said.

"So I see." He lit the cigar, took a puff, exhaled the earthy smoke into the already smoky room. "And from what I hear, up until a week ago I could have turned a pretty penny by handing Raneiro your head."

"That's true," Nico said, pacing the room, picking up objects and setting them down. "But as I'm sure you've heard, I've been given a reprieve of sorts."

Farrell leaned back in his chair. "I did hear. Raneiro must be sending you on some kind of errand."

"You could say that," Nico said.

He wandered back to the chairs in front of Farrell's desk and gestured for Angel to sit. If Farrell wouldn't be a gentlemen, Nico would do it for him. No one was going to make his woman stand while they conducted business.

She sat, and Nico followed suit, taking the seat next to her. Farrell surveyed them behind a steely gaze.

"What can I do for you that Raneiro can't?" Farrell asked.

"I need weapons," Nico said. "And surveillance equipment."

"Sounds right up Raneiro's alley."

"Maybe, but I'd rather be discreet about our movements, and I can't move anything into place without giving them away," Nico said.

Farrell lifted an eyebrow. "And you don't mind telling me?"

Nico shrugged. "It's not ideal, but at this point, I trust you more than I trust Raneiro."

"That might be a mistake," Farrell said.

"It might," Nico agreed. "But there's no help for it."

"You're going to take your chances then?" Farrell asked.

Nico nodded. "I am."

Farrell puffed on the cigar. The bastard enjoyed setting him on edge, making him wait. And he was right; it was a risk. Telling anyone about their plans was a risk. But he had to assume Raneiro would have killed him in Rome if he'd wanted to do so. He obviously wanted the Darknet file badly enough to give Nico the space to procure it. There were no guarantees after that, and keeping some of his movements secret would give him a better chance of getting Angel out alive when all was said and done.

One step at a time.

"Do you have a list of things you need?" Farrell finally asked him.

Nico pulled a folded piece of paper from his pocket and slid it across the metal desk. "We have a logistical problem."

"What's that?"

"I need this stuff in Dublin, and I need to get it there without being detected by law enforcement."

"You know I don't work for free," Farrell said.

"I do."

"How soon?"

"A week," Nico said. "Ten days at the outside."

Farrell studied the list. "I'll do it for a million, wired to my private account." Something that might have passed for a smile touched his lips. "Up front, of course, since your outcome is so... uncertain."

Nico wanted to throttle the bastard. He knew the odds of making it out alive weren't good. Angel probably did, too. But he hated Farrell for saying it out loud in front of her.

"I'll wire it tomorrow," Nico said. "And I'll get you an address as soon as I have one."

Farrell stood. "Good."

They didn't shake hands. Nico waited while Angel stood and then covered her back on the way to the door.

"Was she worth it?"

The question came from behind him. He turned around.

"Yes." It came out more vehemently than he intended. He drew a breath, forced himself to remain calm while he looked at Farrell. "But I guess you'd know all about that, too."

## 27

"What did you mean?" Angel asked Nico while she packed her things for Dublin the next morning. "About Farrell protecting what's his and knowing whether it was worth it?"

Nico placed a stack of shirts in his duffel bag. "Farrell had someone once," he said. "He asked me to help her, and I did."

It was difficult to imagine a man as hard as Farrell Black loving someone that much. But watching Nico, thinking about her own unlikely and immeasurable love for him, Angel guessed no one was immune. They were on their way out of the flat with Luca when a guy in a suit stopped Nico on the street.

"Nico Vitale?"

Nico's hand went immediately to his side, although Angel knew he didn't have a weapon. It was instinct, and he turned his body to cover hers while he faced the guy.

"Who wants to know?"

"This is from Desmond McDermott," the guy said, thrusting an envelope at Nico.

Nico took it, and the guy disappeared into the foot traffic moving down the sidewalk.

"What is it?" Angel asked as Nico tore open the envelope.

He unfolded a piece of paper and studied it. "Looks like a bunch of locations and dates."

"Do they mean anything to you?" Luca asked.

Nico shook his head and folded the piece of paper back into the envelope, then stuffed it in his pocket. "Not right now. Let's go."

They got into the cab and made their way to Heathrow. Angel didn't think about the piece of paper again until they were through security and sitting at the gate, waiting to board the plane.

"We've got awhile yet," Nico said. "I'm going to grab a coffee. Can I get you something?"

Luca put in his headphones. "I'm good."

"I'll take a coffee," Angel said, pulling the tablet out of her bag. "And let me take a look at that piece of paper. I'll do some digging while I wait."

He took the piece of paper out of his pocket and handed it to her, then kissed her head. "Be right back."

She signed into the airport's WIFI and started typing in the locations and dates on the piece of paper. A lot of the places were in the US — Ramona, California, Saddle Brook, New Jersey, Chicago, Illinois — but there was one in the UK (Rochester) and one in Russia (Pskov Region), too. At first they seemed random, but by the time Nico returned carrying two styrofoam cups, the excitement of discovery was buzzing in her mind.

"Here you go," he said, handing her one of the coffees. "Where's Luca?"

"I don't know," she murmured, her eyes still on the screen. "This is interesting…"

"What?" He leaned in.

"These are the dates and locations of major illegal weapons busts," she said, scrolling, her mind trying to formulate the connection she knew was there. "All destined for either everyday criminals or revolutionary warlords."

He took the tablet and looked through the results, a line creasing his forehead.

"What is it?" she asked him.

"Think about it," he said. "Raneiro wants us to get a file called Darknet, which can only be some kind of reference to the online black markets of the same name, then Desmond McDermott gives us a list of illegal weapons busts?"

She sat back in her chair, dread seeping like an oil slick through her veins. "All those rumors about Sean Murdock being involved in illegal drug distribution and weapons…"

He rubbed at the scruff on his chin. "Sean's in the illegal weapons business, and Raneiro wants to take control of it by accessing Sean's client or supply list."

"And he's going to use us to do it." Angel shook her head. She didn't dare think about the consequences. "If we're right - "

"We'll be handing control of a deadly illegal weapons channel to one of the most dangerous men in the world."

# 28

"That Murdock?" Luca asked from the passenger seat.

Nico lifted the binoculars to his eyes and peered at the black car moving toward the iron gates. The windows were tinted, but they'd already run the license plate; it was registered to Sean Murdock's software company and insured against damage under the name of his personal driver.

"Yep," Nico said, still looking through the binoculars.

They'd been casing Murdock's compound outside of Dublin since they arrived in Ireland four days ago. The place was a fortress, enclosed by an electric fence a good foot taller than the one protecting McDermott in Italy. Thanks to Sara's ability to hack into the security company's archives, they knew the property was covered by hi-tech security cameras and flood lights that illuminated the grounds when tripped by a weight of more than ten pounds.

And there were dogs. At least eight of them, all trained to obey Sean Murdock's commands.

Nico passed the binoculars to Luca.

"I don't see how we're going to get in," Luca said as he trained the lenses on the car moving through the front gate.

"I'm working on it," Nico said.

Luca lowered the binoculars, lifted an eyebrow. "You got a plan?"

"More like a wing and a prayer," Nico said. "But I'll let you know when I have more information."

Luca nodded, settled back into the seat of the rental car. "I should be more surprised than I am that this asshole is trading in weapons."

"What do you mean?" Nico asked.

Luca sighed. "Just more evidence that the world is going to hell, that's all."

The pessimism in the statement brought forth a fresh wave of guilt. Nico had befriended Luca when he was a twenty-two-year-old punk without a soul in the world to care whether he lived or died. He had seen Luca's potential and had talked his father into giving Luca a job on the bottom rung. Luca had quickly proven himself loyal and trustworthy and had moved up through the ranks until he was one of the youngest men in the top tier. One of the first things Nico had done when he took over the family was to promote Luca, grooming him for a position as his Underboss. Luca's loyalty was priceless — proven even more in the last year since he'd kidnapped Angel and everything went to hell — but it wasn't a one-way street; Nico had wanted to give Luca a shot at something good, at a life that would be better to him than it had been so far. Instead Luca had grown cynical, carefully insulating himself against any kind of emotion. Nico knew how he felt. Before Angel, he'd been the exact same way. He wondered how long it would take Luca to find the woman who would change his life, make him want more.

"Giving the Darknet file to Raneiro probably isn't going to help," Nico said.

Luca glanced at him. "It's not like he gave you a choice."

"Maybe," Nico said.

He'd been running over their options since Angel found the connection between the file called Darknet and the dates and locations given to them by McDermott's messenger in London. They were already down nine days, which gave them a little over two weeks to steal the file and get it to Raneiro. Nico wanted another option — something that would keep Angel and her brother alive without forcing them to hand over vital, deadly information to Raneiro. An alternate plan had been formulating in the back of his mind, but it wasn't ideal, and it carried its own set of risks. Raneiro wanted the Darknet file, and he wouldn't give them a second chance to get it.

"Still ten guards?" Nico asked.

Luca looked at the notebook in his lap. "By my count. Plus Ian Hayes."

Ian Hayes was Sean Murdock's head of security. He was almost always at the compound, and Nico suspected he lived there. Their initial background check had at first yielded a clean record, but when Sara dug deeper, she turned up arrests for rape, assault, and robbery, all of which had been scrubbed from the official record. Ian had friends in high places — or one at least. However they got into

Murdock's compound, they would have to account for the presence of Ian Hayes.

"How long until we get the delivery from Farrell?" Luca asked.

"Supposed to be sometime in the next week," Nico said.

Luca looked out the window. "We're cutting it close."

Nico raised the binoculars as an SUV approached Murdock's front gate. "Yes, we are."

## 29

They'd been at the cottage in Dublin for more than a week when Angel handed Nico a schedule outlining Sean Murdock's social calendar.

"Murdock's a busy man," Nico murmured.

Angel slid onto his lap at the dining room table and looked at names and dates on the piece of paper. They were hoping to catch Sean with his computer outside the grounds of his home, which was a veritable fortress according to the recon done by Nico and Luca.

"Places to go and people to see," Angel said, kissing Nico's cheek.

He glanced at her. "How did you find all of this?"

"Sara helped with some of it," she said. "The rest was a lot of digging through the social columns in every newspaper and magazine from here to Amsterdam."

Nico returned his gaze to the page in front of him. "I'm still not sure we should try for an off-site event. I know the guy's notoriously protective of his computer, but I don't see him showing up at a black tie affair with a supermodel on one arm and his computer in the other."

Angel shifted a little, felt him grow hard under her ass. "Agreed. But that means breaching the house, and it sounds like it's pretty locked down. I don't know about you, but I'm not crazy about the idea of becoming kibble for those dogs."

He nuzzled her neck. "How about kibble for me?"

She laughed, and her panties grew damp at the feel of his mouth against her skin. "That doesn't sound too bad, but it doesn't sound like a way to get the Darknet file either."

"Good point," he said.

"There is the Clean Water Initiative Fundraiser." She pointed to one of the dates on the list of events. "It's held at Murdock's house."

"Invite only," Nico read from the paper.

"Any strings we could pull?" she asked. "Favors we could call in?"

Footsteps sounded behind them, and she twisted in the chair to see Luca pulling a beer from the fridge.

"Not sure I want to walk into a conversation with the two of you canoodling and talking about an exchange of favors," Luca said, sliding onto one of the dining room chairs with a beer.

"Get your mind out of the gutter," Angel said. "We're talking about securing an invite to a fundraiser held at Murdock's house."

Luca leaned forward. "Is that possible?"

Nico rubbed his forehead, and Angel felt a pang of concern as she saw the fatigue in his eyes. He and Luca did recon at all hours of the day and night. When Nico was home, Angel would often wake in the middle of the night to find him sitting at the dining room table in the dark, his forehead creased with worry. The only time he seemed at peace was when they made love. They were both free then, lost in the passion that burned so hot between them that it obliterated everything else in its path.

"A year ago, yes," Nico said. "But MediaComm has been in the hands of an interim CEO since my reported death. It's not like I have any official standing to lean on."

It wasn't their only problem. What if the Darknet file wasn't on the computer they found? What if they were caught? What if Raneiro had them killed anyway?

Then again, none of those things mattered if they couldn't find a way to get close to Murdock's computer. She was relieved when Luca changed the subject.

"So the delivery from Farrell is still on for tomorrow?"

Nico nodded. "As far as I know."

"Do we trust Farrell to deliver without tipping off the police?"

Nico's jaw tightened. "We don't have a choice."

Angel kissed his cheek and slid off his lap. "I'm going to use one of the Tracphones to call David."

They hadn't used the landline in the cottage. It was a precautionary measure, but after the incident in Rome with Sean Murdock's men, they were all of the "better safe than sorry" mindset.

"Tell him and Sara hello," Nico said.

"Will do."

She went into the bedroom they shared and pulled one of the phones from her bag, then sat on the bed as she dialed. David picked up on the first ring.

"Hey, sis."

"Hey. How are you?" she asked.

"Good," he said. "Really good."

"Yeah?"

"Yeah." She could hear his smile through the phone. "How are you?"

"Hanging in there," she said.

"Where are you right now?"

"I'd rather not say." No one but Sara knew about Nico's island in Maine, and the Tracphones were an added precaution, but she didn't want to take any chances.

"Got it," he said. "Very mysterious."

"Just careful," she said.

"When will you be back?" he asked.

She plucked at a hole in her jeans. "I don't know."

"Can you at least tell me if you have a plan for dealing with Raneiro?"

"We do," she said, "but I'm not happy about it."

"Why?"

"Because it means giving him something dangerous, and it means letting him off the hook for what he's done to us."

"I can't speak to the first thing," David said, "but do you really care about the second?"

"What do you mean?"

He sighed. "I don't know, Ange... I mean, I'm not exactly a fan of the guy, but don't we just want to start over? Isn't that what matters at this point?"

"Is that what matters to you?"

He hesitated. "I think so."

"What would that mean?" she asked him.

He laughed. "I haven't really gotten that far. But I don't think I can go back to school, pretend none of his happened, pick up where I left off."

"So what then?"

"Maybe start over someplace new? See where life takes us? It's not like we don't have money."

He was right, but somehow it didn't feel that simple. The thought of letting Raneiro off the hook, letting him walk away — not only with the Darknet file but without paying for what he'd done to her and David and Nico — turned her stomach.

*... it's going to come down to life or revenge. I know what I want most. Do you?*

Nico's words drifted through her mind. She still didn't have an answer.

"I guess," she finally said.

"You don't sound convinced," he said.

"I'm not."

"Why, Ange?" His voice was soft, and she had to swallow the lump that rose in her throat.

"Because it's not fair," she said, more vehemently than she'd intended.

"I agree," he said. But if we don't try to move on, what's the point? Isn't that what we're fighting for?"

The words sat between them. What he said made sense. So why wasn't she sure she could live with the idea of Raneiro getting away with what he'd done?

"I just wanted to check in," she said. She wanted to get off the phone, away from the questions that felt like a knife digging into the wounds she thought had healed. "I'm glad you're doing so well."

"I hope you're doing okay, too," he said. "I worry about you."

"Don't. I'm fine. Just keep getting better, and I'll see you soon."

"Sounds good. Love you, Ange. Take care."

"You, too."

She disconnected the call and looked down at the phone in her hands, David's words ringing through her ears.

*Isn't that what we're fighting for?*

# 30

It was around noon the next day when Nico and Luca pulled into the driveway. They'd left early that morning to pick up the supplies from Farrell Black's man down by the waterfront, and while Angel had wanted to go, even she couldn't argue that the task didn't require three of them. She'd stayed behind instead, nervously watching the clock, hoping Farrell hadn't double-crossed them by tipping off the police that they were bringing weapons into the country.

She didn't know whether to be relieved or disappointed when Nico and Luca pulled two small cases from the back of the car. On the one hand, maybe it meant they weren't expecting a lot of resistance at Murdock's.

On the other hand, what if they were wrong?

They brought everything into the living room and cracked open the locks on the big, black cases with a pair of bolt cutters. Angel catalogued while they called out everything in the cases, being careful to note not only the kind of item but the quantity so they'd have a good sense what they had to work with.

She'd gotten used to being around guns, even if she never actually grew to like them, but these were weapons of a different sort — handguns but also semi-automatics with silencers and huge magazines. And not just weapons. There were body cams like the ones they'd used in LA, mini-cameras, kevlar, and night vision goggles. She pushed aside the fear that rose in her at the sight of it all, too familiar after the fiasco in LA. They might not need everything that was here, but it was better to be prepared. At least this time David's life wouldn't be hanging in the balance.

They were finishing up lunch when Angel started to get the feeling Nico had something on his mind. She knew him too well now, was familiar with his nervous tells — his tendency to turn his wine glass while deep in thought, to avoid her eyes. She waited, giving him the space he obviously needed.

"I think I might have a plan for getting an invite to the CWI fundraiser," he finally said.

She leaned against the counter and folded her arms over her chest. "Why do I have a feeling I'm not going to like it?"

"You're not," he said.

Luca took a drink of his wine and stayed quiet.

She sighed. "You might as well tell me." He'd do what he wanted anyway. She knew that, and knew, too, that it was something they had in common.

"If I give a press conference announcing I'm alive, I can use MediaComm to get an invitation. I'll be at the top of everyone's guest list, if only because they'll be morbidly curious about my fake death."

She shook her head. "You might as well paint a target on your back. Everyone who was with Dante will know you're alive."

"If Farrell Black is any indication," he said, "everyone in the Syndicate already knows."

She cast around in her mind for another excuse to veto the idea. Right now, Nico was a ghost. It didn't make him bullet proof, but it did offer an extra layer of protection against anyone who might mean him harm.

"If you give a press conference, the paparazzi will be all over us. How are we supposed to move around in secret?"

"We can make it a press release," he said. "Run it through the company. We don't have to disclose our location. It's not like we've been social here in Dublin."

She bit her lip. He was right. They'd played it low key, spending most of their time in the cottage they'd rented outside the city. The only people who knew they were there was Farrell Black, and he'd already proven he could be trusted by coming through with the supplies they needed.

"Won't Murdock be hesitant to let you on his property after his henchman warned you off in Rome?" Luca asked.

"Maybe," Nico said. "But the guest list is probably handled by some event planner. As the CEO of MediaComm, especially one who just made a big announcement, I'll be a prime guest for a fundraiser. And all that attention on me means you and Angel will be more free to move around."

Luca looked surprised. "Me? How am I getting in?"

"I'll give you a big MediaComm title. Angel will be a plus one."

The plan wasn't unfamiliar; they'd done something similar at John Lando's house in LA before rescuing David. The party had been well-attended by John's movie industry friends, and his Underboss had been so focused on Nico that he hadn't bothered to watch Angel as she slipped from the crowd to give Sara remote access to John's computer. The data they'd gotten from it had ultimately helped them figure out where Dante was keeping David. It had been terrifying. But it had worked.

"What about Raneiro?" Angel asked. "Think it will tip him off that we're in Dublin?"

"Raneiro knows this is Sean's home turf," Nico said. "We have a little over two weeks until his deadline. He has to know we're here somewhere."

The thought didn't bring her any comfort.

"He's right," Luca said. "In a perfect world, Nico could stay invisible until this thing with Murdock is done. But this might be our only way to get onto Murdock's property. and there might be another upside."

"What's that?" Angel asked.

"Letting everyone know Nico's alive makes him more visible. If anything, it might offer him extra protection against a double-cross by Raneiro, at least in the short term."

It wasn't entirely untrue. If Nico told the world he was alive, the spotlight would be so bright on him that it might offer him a measure of protection. Maybe not forever, but at least until they could get the Darknet file off Sean Murdock's computer.

"I guess I see your point," she admitted.

"Good." Nico crossed the room, tucked a piece of hair behind her ear, touched his mouth gently to hers. "It will be okay."

She wanted to believe him. If anyone could make everything okay, it was Nico. But she couldn't help feeling that there were too many pieces in play. And that the events set in motion were already well out of their control.

# 31

Nico sat in one of the chairs in the cavernous knave of Christ Church. It was one of his favorites, built around 1030 and steeped in the kind of history that just wasn't present in the US. It was a low key tourist attraction, and a couple of people moved through the church, stopping to take pictures. He ran his eyes over them, checking for signs that they might mean him harm. But they were just people, sightseeing or doing research or simply taking a walk.

He let his gaze roam the soaring barrel ceiling as he moved the rosary between his fingers. The meeting that was about to take place would change everything.

Then again, things had already changed. It was time to accept that nothing would ever be the same, that if he and Angel wanted a chance at a normal life, they would have to build it from the ground up. There was no going back.

*Angel...*

He hated seeing her in pain, and she would hate it if she knew he could see it. She took pride in her strength. He didn't want to take that from her. But he saw the trauma that lurked in her eyes when they talked about David, about the four months she'd thought Nico was dead. Worst of all was watching her try to cover it up, so afraid to show she was hurting that she piled hatred and anger on top of her pain in an attempt to stuff it down. He knew all about that, knew that hardening your heart only made it crack wider and more permanently when it finally did.

He didn't want that for her. He wanted her to be happy and free. To live with all the spirit and optimism she had when they'd first met. That he'd been party to taking that from her was something he would never forgive himself for. But he could try to make it right. Could try to give her another chance. He could only hope she was willing to choose peace over vengeance.

He glanced over as a man in jeans and a sweater sat next to him, then returned his eyes to the front of the church. Nico was still moving through the beads in his hand when the man spoke.

"I hope you called for more than a prayer partner," Agent Braden Kane said.

"It can't hurt," Nico said.

"I agree. But Ireland's a long way from New York just for prayer."

"The distance couldn't be helped."

"I thought you were dead," Kane said.

"You and everyone else."

Kane leaned back in the chair. "Faking your death is a felony."

"I think you have bigger fish to fry."

"What kind of fish are we talking about?" he asked.

Nico looked down at the rosary in his hands. "Full cooperation."

Kane sat forward, clasped his hands in front of his body. "Are you kidding?"

Nico shook his head. "This is no joking matter."

"What are we talking about?" Kane asked.

"Information on the Syndicate's high-level activities, specifically those run by Raneiro Donati, plus proof that he and Sean Murdock are involved in illegal weapons sales."

Kane let out a low whistle. "We've been tracking Murdock for awhile. And you know how long we've wanted Donati."

Nico nodded. "There are conditions."

"What kind of conditions?"

"Amnesty for myself, Angelica Rossi, David Rossi, Luca Cassano, and everyone in the Vitale family."

"I can't promise that," Kane said.

Nico stood. "Then we don't have a deal."

Kane put a hand on Nico's arm. "Wait. Sit. Let's finish this."

Nico sat. "It's non-negotiable. You know we're not into the hard stuff. The people who work for me are no more dangerous than the traders on Wall Street."

"I'm going to need something pretty compelling to sell that upline," Kane said.

"How about a list of illegal weapons suppliers? Or maybe the names of clients cultivated by one of the world's richest and most upstanding entrepreneurs?"

"You have something like that?" Kane asked.

"I will. And proof that Donati plans to take over the supply chain."

"You and the Rossis and Cassano looking for protection afterwards?"

"That won't be necessary," Nico said. "We can take care of ourselves. We just want to walk when it's all said and done, and I need assurances that my people will walk, too."

"This is big," he said.

"It is."

"What kind of timeline are we talking about here?" Kane asked.

"I need to know within a week," Nico said. "I'll have the proof to you within two."

Kane drew a deep breath. "I'll see what I can do. Where can I reach you?"

"You can't." Nico stood. "I'll call you in a couple of days."

He stepped around Kane and made his way out of the church without looking back.

## 32

Angel used her foot to turn on the hot water, then sunk lower in the bath while it got warmer. After two glasses of wine and almost an hour in the tub, she was slightly drowsy, her body loose and relaxed. Luca and Nico had gone out for a beer, but she'd been unusually tired and had opted instead for a couple of hours alone with some candles and the giant, old tub in the cottage's master bathroom.

She wondered again what Nico had been up to earlier in the day. It wasn't unusual for him not to tell her where he was going or what he was doing, but she'd gotten good at sensing when it was because he was hiding something.

And he was definitely hiding something.

She reached for the tap with her foot and turned off the hot water. Nico would tell her when he was ready, like he always did. Trusting someone so much was a revelation. And she did trust him. With her safety. Her body. Her life.

She closed her eyes, imagined his hands on her, the feel of his lips, soft as velvet on her sex. One hand snaked almost unbidden down her stomach, and she let her legs fall open, her breath catching in her throat at the thought of him nestled between her thighs, pushing into her.

"Starting without me?"

The words caught her by surprise, and her eyes flew open as she sat up, instinctively covering her breasts. Then she saw Nico standing in the doorway, eyes like liquid gold in the candle light, his mouth turned up into a sly smile.

She sank back into the water. "You scared me."

"I'm sorry." He didn't move, just raised his eyebrows. "So? Were you?"

She grinned. "Just thinking about you actually."

"Oh, really?"

"Hm-mmm."

"I think I like the sound of that." He crossed the room, sat on the edge of the tub, dipped his hand in the water.

"You want to come in?" she asked.

"Is that metaphorical?"

She smiled. "Maybe."

He rested his hand on her knee, ran it up her thigh under the water, seemingly oblivious to the fact that his rolled shirt sleeves were getting wet.

"Then yes," he said. "I'd like to come in."

Her nipples rose to points over the lapping water, and she opened her thighs for him as his hand snaked higher. "Then come in."

He growled, reaching for her hand, and pulled her up out of the water. She thought he would give her a towel. Instead he scooped her up into his arms, and grabbed the bottle of wine on the counter. Then he made for the bedroom.

She laughed. "I'm getting you all wet!"

"I know," he said. "Now it's your turn."

He dropped her onto the bed and set the wine on the nightstand, his eyes predatory as he unbuttoned his shirt, took off his pants. Then he was naked in front of her, his body as sculpted as a gladiator, the perfectly formed chest giving way to the corded muscle of his abs, the taut skin of his stomach leading to the cock that hung, heavy and engorged, just for her.

His eyes hungrily roamed her dripping body. "You're so beautiful."

"I was going to say the same thing to you," she said, her voice throaty.

He grinned, then prowled to the bed like an animal cornering its prey. He climbed up over her body. His shaft rested against the inside of her thigh, and the feel of his naked skin, hot and smooth against the cool slickness of her own, sent a rush of wetness to her center.

He lowered his lips to one of her breasts and covered the nipple with his mouth. The heat of it against the sensitive bud made her gasp, and she arched her back, wanting him to take it all. The tip of his cock nudged against her core, and she opened her legs, reaching for him, wanting him inside her.

He chuckled, low and sexy, and moved her hand away. "Not yet, baby. I'm nowhere near done with you."

He pinned her hands over her head and moved above her, letting his cock tease her clit until she moved under him, working the angle for her own pleasure. He licked her lower lip, pulling away when she tried to capture his tongue in her mouth, teasing until she moaned with frustration.

He let go of one of her hands to cup her other breast, running the thick pad of his thumb over the tight peak while he covered her mouth with his own, his tongue stroking her mouth like a finely tuned instrument, making her wetter and hotter for him as she imagined his mouth on her, his cock inside her.

She ran her free hand down his stomach, reaching for him. She sighed when she finally had him in her palm, and she felt him grow bigger as she stroked, moving her hand in time to the rhythm of their mouths, exploring each other like it was the first time.

He captured her wrist, pulled it away from him. "You're being very impatient tonight."

"I want you," she gasped.

And she did. She was slick with desire, her pussy desperate for the completion that only he could give her.

"And you'll have me," he said hoarsely. "But I'm going to have to keep your hands out of the way for a bit longer."

He held her wrists with one hand while he reached for the nightstand with another. When he came back, he was holding one of his ties, and he used it to secure her wrists to the iron headboard.

"You're tying me up now?" she asked, laughing a little.

"I told you to be a good girl and wait," he said. "But since you're so demanding tonight, I think I'll have to cover your eyes in order to really have my way with you."

"Don't be ridiculous," she said.

But he got up from the bed, his cock swinging in all its magnificent glory from the perfection of his body, and retrieved another tie from the dresser. "I assure you that I'm very, very serious."

He came back to the bed, straddling her. "Unless you don't want me to."

She smiled. There were a lot of things she wasn't sure about, especially now. She didn't know what the future held, didn't know if they would even make it out of Dublin alive, let alone get away from Raneiro Donati when it was all over.

But Nico would never hurt her. She knew that as sure as she knew the sun would rise in the east.

"Go ahead," she said softly. "I trust you."

He bent his head to hers, kissed her gently before slipping his tongue inside her mouth, bringing her body to the height of passion all over again. Then he wrapped the tie around her eyes and knotted it behind her head.

She was instantly plunged into darkness, the sensation at once terrifying and exciting. She could feel Nico's body over hers, feel the weight of his cock on her belly as he slid down between her legs, but she had no visual cues to guess what would come next. Her senses were heightened, every brush of his skin on hers electric.

She felt his body angle away from hers for a minute, and then a cool trickle of liquid on her breast. Wine, she realized. He was pouring wine on her body, and she gasped as his tongue lapped at the liquid, closing around the nipple, sucking while he squeezed the other one. She moaned, her pussy throbbing as he moved down her stomach.

For a few seconds, there was nothing, then something cold as more wine filled her belly button. She groaned as he clutched her hips, opening his mouth to her stomach, sucking the wine from her, his mouth close enough to her pussy that it wasn't hard to imagine the feel of his tongue sliding into her, closing over her clit, sucking until she came.

She tugged at the tie binding her hands. "I want to touch you."

"Not yet," he said, moving lower.

He spread her thighs with his big hands, and she felt the cool rush of liquid over her sex. Her back came up off the bed as his mouth covered her pussy, heating the cool wine while he lapped it from her slippery folds.

"Nico..."

She opened her legs wider, wanting him to taste all of her. As if answering the call of her body, he slid his tongue through the engorged petals, thrusting it up into her until she groaned, her climax a storm on the horizon.

He pulled his mouth away and slid his fingers inside her. "You're sweeter than wine, baby. I could drink you all day."

The words were spoken into her darkness. There was nothing but his voice, smokey and loaded with sex, and his fingers inside her, his thumb making circles over her clit.

"I can feel you getting ready to come," he said. "And I'm going to make you come harder than you've ever come before."

He pulled his fingers out, and a moment later, he was pressing against the bud of her asshole.

She startled, and he spoke softly. "Is it okay?"

She leaned back, gave herself over to the sensation, let go of her inhibitions, let her body answer the question for her. "Yes."

He eased his pinky, slick with her juices, inside her. She relaxed, letting her body open to him. He didn't move at all at first, and a few seconds later, his mouth was on her pussy again. The sensation was exquisite — his mouth slipping through her while his fingers slowly penetrated her ass. Lost in the darkness, her body had a mind of it's own now, and she moved against his mouth, pushing her pussy against his tongue while he worked her ass with his finger. She felt the rumbling of a powerful orgasm at her center, an earthquake threatening to tear her apart, and she cried out as he slipped a bigger finger inside her, working with the rhythm of his mouth to create a sensation so powerfully erotic, the force of it almost frightened her.

But she didn't have time to be scared. Her body took over under the gentle coaxing of Nico's hands and mouth, opening to him like a flower in the sun until she couldn't have stopped if she'd tried. She pushed down on his hand, giving herself over to the ecstasy of his penetrating finger against the silken feel of his mouth lapping at her pussy and clit.

The storm broke inside her body all at once, sending a bolt of lightening cracking through her center. She cried out, tugging against the restraints on her wrists, the headboard clattering against the wall as she came against his mouth, the orgasm rushing like wave after wave inside her body.

When she finally stopped shuddering, Nico's body moved over hers. Then the candlelit room came into view, and he untied her wrists. She took advantage of his momentary distraction to slide out from under him, pushing him back onto the bed and straddling his body.

She lowered her face over his, her hair a curtain that blocked out the rest of the world. "What did you do to me?"

She didn't give him time to answer before she lowered her mouth to his. Tasting her sex on his lips sent a sensual lick of heat through her body, and she slid over his insistent cock, letting it slip through the crevices of her soaking wet pussy.

He groaned in her mouth, and she moved her lips down the stubble on his chin. She continued to his neck and chest, feathering kisses over the god-like ridges of his chest on her way down his stomach.

He took hold of her shoulders. "I need to fuck you."

She laughed. "You think I'm going to let you off that easy after what you just did to me?"

She settled between his legs, took his magnificent cock in her hands, relishing the powerful weight of it. She stroked him soft and slow with one hand while she took his balls in the other, then flicked her tongue against his tip. He shuddered, and she closed her mouth around the thick crown and sucked before sliding her mouth down his shaft all at once.

He gasped, and he stroked her hair, pulled it away from her face. When she looked up at him, he was watching her, a complicated brew of lust and love etched on his face. She took him to the back of her throat while she looked at him, and his head fell back against the pillow.

"Fuck, Angel. You feel so good."

She worked the base of him with one hand while she slid back up, sucking on the tip before sinking back onto him. He pumped his hips against her mouth, thighs flexing, his arousal tugging at her insides until she was on fire for him all over again.

"Come here, baby," he gasped. "Ride me."

She wanted to follow his instructions, but she wanted to taste him more, and she worked his cock faster with her mouth and her hand, making sure he knew that she had no intention of leaving until he came.

"Fuck... I'm going to come if you don't get up here right now, Angel."

His cock was huge, swollen and rigid in her mouth, getting bigger and harder by the second as he came closer to climax. She reveled in the power to bring him the kind of bliss he brought her, and she tightened her grip, sucked harder.

He growled, and a second later he was spilling into her mouth, the hot liquid sliding down her throat, making them one in yet another way. She didn't stop until she'd licked him clean. Then she collapsed against his body, her head on his chest.

He leaned down, captured her mouth in his, kissed her long and deep. "You're amazing."

She sighed. "Back at you."

# 33

"That wasn't a rhetorical question," she said later.

Two hours later they were still in bed, her naked body pressed against Nico's in the fading candlelight, her head on his chest. He stroked her hair.

"What wasn't?"

She rested her head on his chest and looked up at him. "I want to know what you did to me."

He laughed, bent his head to kiss her. "If I remember correctly, I made you come like a freight train. And then after you did the same to me, I fucked you and made you come again."

"That pretty much sums it up." She sighed. "This is all I want. Just you and me and a bed forever and ever."

He continued stroking her head, but she sensed something go still in him. He spoke a moment later.

"We could have it."

"I hope you're right," she said.

"No," he said. "I think I've figured out a way for us to get out of this alive."

"You mean me weren't going to get out of it alive before?"

"There have always been risks, and risks for afterwards, too," he said softly.

"You never really believed that Raneiro would let us go," she said.

"I hoped he would, but I also knew we'd be looking over our shoulders for the rest of our lives."

"And now?" she asked.

"Now I think I might have come up with a solution."

She put a little space between him so she could see his face. "I'm listening."

He drew in a breath. "A couple years ago, I was approached by someone from the FBI…"

She sat up. "The FBI?"

He nodded.

She almost thought she'd heard him wrong. Almost. "Are you talking about selling out the Syndicate?"

"It's not my first choice, but I'm not seeing a better way out here."

She shook her head. "So, what? We'd hand over a bunch of Syndicate secrets to the Feds and they'd let us go?"

"More or less," he said.

"What about Luca? And Sara? And Marco and Elia?" She looked away, the magnitude of what he was suggesting really hitting her. "We'd be traitors. Doesn't the Syndicate kill people for that?"

He sat up next to her. "There wouldn't be anybody left to come after us. We'd give them Raneiro, everyone at the top, and they'd give amnesty to our people."

"Can they do that?" she asked.

"My cooperation would be contingent on it," he said.

"What would happen after it was all over? Would we go into Witness Protection or something?" She tried to imagine it — Nico and David and her living under the watchful eyes of the FBI for the rest of their lives.

"We'd make our own way," he said. "I have plenty of money stashed, and I'm at least as confident in my ability to keep us alive as I am in the Feds. The head of the snake will be gone. The Syndicate will be in ruins. We'd be okay."

"What about the Darknet file?"

"We can hand that over, too. They would bury Raneiro with it, and probably Murdock. We'd be getting some really bad guys off the street, and the FBI could use the file to track people involved with weapons trafficking, people who are completely under the radar right now. We'd be doing a good thing."

"So Raneiro would spend the rest of his life in prison?" she asked.

"Most likely."

"Most likely..." she repeated.

Most likely wasn't good enough. She wanted to bury Raneiro for what he'd done, and although she hadn't admitted it out loud, she realized now that she'd always envisioned it happening through his death. Handing him over to the Feds meant prison, or worse, the possibility of him walking on a technicality.

"I know it's not a guarantee, but Angel... I want to keep you alive more than I want to see him dead. I want more nights like this one. I want to see David recover and live his life, and I want to see you happy and free."

"And you think working with the Feds would do all of that?"

He sighed. "I think it's the least shitty option out of all the shitty options we have to choose from."

"Is this something you've already decided?" she asked.

"Not necessarily, no. I've reached out to my FBI contact to see if it's even possible under these terms, but I wanted to talk to you before I made a decision."

"Let me think about it." She hated herself for saying it. It should have been an easy decision: an almost-sure way to have a new life with Nico and David versus possible death at the hands of Raneiro Donati — now or later.

But she was finding it wasn't as easy to let go of anger, of bitterness, as people wanted you to believe. After awhile, the fortress you built to shelter all that rage got bigger and stronger. Maybe it wasn't even possible to break it down anymore.

"Okay," Nico said. "But think fast. Murdock's fundraiser is in less than two weeks."

## 34

"How bad is it?" Angel turned around on the sofa as Nico came into the living room.

He'd been on the phone on and off for twenty-four hours, first to explain to the MediaComm board that he was alive and well and then to issue orders for the press release that would alert the media. Unfortunately, word got out ahead of the release, and now the PR people at MediaComm were working double time to get in front of the concerns raised by investors.

"No worse than expected," he said, sitting next to her.

"Will it hurt the company's stock?" Luca asked from a chair across the room.

"Don't know, don't care," Nico said. "The last four months were a death knell for my time at MediaComm. I'll let the board appoint someone new and sell my controlling interest. They can have it. It was only ever a cover for the Syndicate anyway."

He was surprised to find that it was true, that he didn't care. A year ago, his life had been orderly and profitable, with two businesses operating at optimal efficiency and profitability. Now he was on the run, forced to give up the operation he'd grown as an homage to his father and contemplating turning against the Syndicate. But all of that paled in comparison to the importance of the woman sitting next to him. Somehow she'd become his whole life, and he would have sacrificed everything a hundred times over to have her.

Angel took his hand. "Are you okay?" she asked softly.

He opened her fingers, kissed her palm. "I have you. I'll always be okay as long as that's true."

Luca cleared his throat. "How long do you think we have before the press finds you?"

"Awhile yet," Nico said. "No one knows we're here, not even Sara or David. As long as we lay low, be careful when we go out, we should be okay. We'll have to move on after the fundraiser though. There might be paparazzi outside Murdock's property. We don't want them following us back here."

"We'll need to move on anyway if we don't want Murdock to come after us when he realizes the file is missing," Luca said.

Nico nodded. "We'll set it up so we can leave the country straight from the fundraiser."

"What's our plan for getting the file?" Angel asked. "Not being able to get inside the compound ahead of the event will hurt us, won't it?"

"It's not ideal," Nico admitted. "But we have floor plans from the company that handled Murdock's renovation of the house, and we have that article you read in Architectural Digest. My hunch is that Murdock's computer is in that study."

"Do we have any idea how difficult it will be to access?" she asked.

"Not really," he said.

"She should learn to use a lock pick just in case," Luca suggested.

Nico rubbed a tired hand over his face, fighting the pull of exhaustion. "I'm still not crazy about Angel copying the file."

"I know," Luca said. "But you can't do it — Murdock's people will be watching you. And it makes more sense for me to keep watch in case she runs into trouble inside the study."

Nico nodded. "I know. I just wish there were another way."

Angel kissed his cheek. "I'll be fine. I got to John Lando's computer, didn't I?"

"Don't fool yourself into thinking this will be the same thing." He wanted her to know the operation was dangerous, and he secretly still hoped she would change her mind and agree to stay behind. It was a foolish wish. She would never let him and Luca go in alone. "Murdock is a bit of a paranoid genius. He's cagey about his personal space, and this isn't an intimate party for a few friends. There will be over two hundred people there, and that means a lot of guards, a lot of security."

"I can handle it," she said.

She said it without an ounce of uncertainty. It should have made him feel better — like she was really ready. But it only made him worry more. It had been two days since their conversation about the FBI. She hadn't said any more about it, but the fact that she had to consider whether she would rather hand Raneiro over to the Feds so they could make a clean getaway or risk not getting away at all to take down Raneiro themselves told him all he needed to know; she was still holding onto her pain.

And he knew from experience that pain could make you reckless.

"Should we bring in Marco and Elia?" Luca asked, pulling him away from his thoughts.

"I don't think we can get them in," Nico said.

"Maybe, but we could use them outside the gates in case things go south," Luca said.

"That's true," Nico said.

His phone buzzed and he took it out, looked at the display, and read the text from Jenna, who had been every bit as surprised to learn he was alive as everyone at MediaComm. As his former personal assistant, she had left the family after his supposed death and was now working at an advertising firm in the city, but they went way back. She'd been more than happy to make a few calls on his behalf.

"Good news," Nico said, slipping the phone back in his pocket. "The invitation to Murdock's fundraiser came through. We're good to go."

Angel sighed. "Then I guess I'm going to need another dress."

## 35

Angel was putting her clothes back on in the dressing room of a downtown boutique when she started to feel sick. The wave of nausea rolled through her, and she sat on the stool in the luxurious dressing room, swallowing the bile that rose in her throat.

She'd been relieved when Nico had allowed her to go shopping without him or Luca. She loved them, but after nearly two weeks in the Dublin cottage, she was feeling stifled. She wanted to stretch her legs, breathe some fresh air. And she wanted to do it without feeling like a princess who couldn't go shopping by herself. Nico hadn't liked it, but he'd given her one of the guns from Farrell and told her to be back by five unless she wanted him to come looking.

"Is everything all right?" the saleswoman asked from outside the door.

"Fine." Angel drew in a breath and reached for the gray-green dress by Louise Kennedy that hung on a hook behind her. She opened the door a crack and passed it through. "I'll take this one, please."

"Very good." The woman had the same charming lilt Angel had heard in passing conversation around the city. If shock hadn't already turned her cheeks hot, she might even have smiled.

But there was shock, because if she was right...

She did the math; she was almost two weeks late for her period.

She touched a hand to her brow, trying to remember all the times she and Nico had sex since she'd found out he was alive. It was true they'd slipped up a couple of times before the fiasco in LA. The way they'd been living — on the run, in fear for their lives, trying to rescue David — hadn't made it easy to keep practical matters at the front of their minds. She flashed back to the time Nico had taken her on the beach below Locke's house, his breath mingling with the brine of the sea as he drove into her. They hadn't used a condom then, and she'd almost hoped she was pregnant in the weeks after his funeral.

But they'd been careful since he'd come back. Hadn't they?

She backtracked through their time together, trying to remember if she'd seen him grab a condom through the desire-fueled haze that spread through her like wildfire when he touched her. Had he used a condom in Maine the first time they'd been together again? The night was a blur of shock and bliss and relief. She remembered his mouth on hers, his hair in her hands, the feel of his body — so solid, so real. But she didn't remember a condom.

And anyway, it didn't matter. Birth control wasn't foolproof. She was late. It was at least possible.

She took a deep breath as the nausea passed and left the dressing room. Then she paid for the dress, asked the saleswoman where she might find a pharmacy, and put her wallet away with trembling hands.

A complex storm of emotion brewed in mind as she made her way farther uptown. This wasn't what some people would call good timing. They were still putting the finishing touches on their plans to infiltrate Sean Murdock's study during the fundraiser next week. She hadn't decided what to do about the FBI. Then there was the handover to Raneiro. Would they even make it out of it alive?

There was no way to know what the future held. So why did she feel a tiny spark of something like hope? Something like joy? What would it be like to carry Nico's child? To share something so profound? To have a child that would be the very best of both of them?

She shook her head. It might not be true. Being late didn't mean she was pregnant. She'd been under a lot of stress lately, had been traveling all over the place. She just needed to find out for sure to ease her mind. Then she could get back to focusing on the fundraiser. And she needed to focus, because right now their plans were about as low-tech and risky as they could get — attend the fundraiser, pick the lock to Sean's study, hope his computer was there, hope it had the Darknet file, hope she could steal it undetected. A million things could go wrong, but they weren't trained spies, and they hadn't had the benefit of casing the interior of Sean's compound. It was the best they could do with the time they had.

Thinking about the details made her feel better. She was just a little tired, that's all. She didn't have time to be pregnant. Maybe later, if she and Nico made it out alive, if they were able to start over somewhere. But not right now. She'd get the pregnancy test, find out for sure, and get back to work. She felt better already.

## 36

Two hours later she was sitting on the toilet seat, looking at the white stick with the two pink lines. She almost couldn't believe it. She was pregnant, and while she would need a doctor to confirm it, something deep inside her knew it was true. She'd been tired. Tired and a little under the weather. Food she usually liked didn't taste right, and she found herself craving things that typically didn't appeal to her. She put a hand against her breasts through her shirt. They were full and tender.

She was pregnant with Nico's baby.

The knowledge sent a powerful burst of happiness through her, as surprising as a warm summer wind. She imagined telling Nico, knew with certainty that he would be thrilled in spite of the circumstances.

But then he would want to protect her. Would send her back to Maine to wait with David and Sara while he and Luca dealt with Raneiro. And while there might have been a time when she would have been okay with that kind of arrangement, she wasn't that person anymore. Nico had been taken from her once. She wouldn't send him to face the Syndicate alone.

And what about the FBI? There was no doubt in her mind that once Nico knew she was pregnant, he would push even harder to work with them. She wasn't stupid. She knew there were advantages to doing so. They would have tactical support and backup during the handover of the Darknet file to Raneiro — assuming they could even get it off Sean Murdock's computer. They could probably even arrange to have their personal information kept hidden from anyone who might come looking for them when they tried to disappear.

But it also meant giving up the certainty that Raneiro Donati would have to answer in any meaningful way for what he'd done. It meant giving justice over to someone else and hoping for the best, instead of exacting it herself when she could be sure he'd really pay.

She thought about all the data she'd gathered on the men who had betrayed Nico. What would happen to them? She hadn't developed a plan for going back to Boston and finishing what she'd started, but somehow she'd thought she was hitting the Pause button on her plans for revenge. Working with the FBI meant committing to a future she hadn't dared consider. Was she willing to let go of the past and step into the future? Was she even capable of doing it after all that had happened?

A knock on the door shook her from her thoughts.

"Angel?" Nico's voice. "You okay?"

"I'm good," she said, slipping the pregnancy test inside her jeans. She flattened the package and buried it under the bathroom trash, then rinsed her hands and opened the door. "Hey, you're back."

He and Luca had left the cottage to contact Marco and Elia through some kind of anonymous email channel they had set up for just such a purpose.

"And so are you." He slid his arms around her waist and looked down into her eyes. For a minute, she was sure he could see her secret, that he could see right through her skin and bones to the heart of everything she was and everything she wasn't sure she could be anymore. "How did it go?"

Panic raced through her body like a lit fuse. Did he know about the pregnancy test?

He smiled. "The dress?"

"Oh… right. The dress."

He tipped his head, like he was trying to figure something out. "Are you sure you're okay?"

"I'm fine," she said. "Just a little tired."

"So? Did you find something for the fundraiser?" he asked.

"I did. Although…"

He lifted his eyebrows in silent question.

"Well, I never thought I'd say this, but I'm kind of hoping I don't have to do any dress shopping anytime soon."

He laughed. "Even the fun stuff gets old after awhile I guess."

She grinned as his hands cupped her ass. "Not all of it."

And it was true. Even now, tired and with her newfound secret between them, she wanted him, the familiar pull of longing tugging between her thighs, making her wet.

He lowered his head until she could feel his breath — clean and sweet — against her lips. "I should hope not."

He brought his mouth to hers and kissed her deep and slow. She let her hands roam the wide plane of his back, felt his fingers at the crevice of her ass, close enough to her core to make her ache for him. His tongue slipped into her mouth, and an answering surge of moisture soaked her panties. She was pressed flat against his body, enveloped by his big arms, feeling as safe as she ever felt. She had a sudden desire to tell him everything. Come clean about the baby and all her fears.

He pulled away, smoothed the hair at the crown of her head. "You sure you want to do this?" he asked. "You could go back to Maine. Wait with David and Sara."

She hated that he'd spent so much of the last year worrying about her. And he didn't need to. She'd had four months to harden her heart against their enemies, to prepare for what was coming. There was no point thinking about the future, trying to protect something that didn't exist as long as Raneiro Donati ran the Syndicate. She would tell him about the baby when it was over. When they could really celebrate their future together.

One thing at a time.

"No way," she said, smiling up at him. "You're not going to have all the fun without me."

He returned her smile, but she saw a shadow cross his eyes and knew she'd made the right decision. He didn't need any more reasons to worry about her. Whatever was coming, she could handle it.

# 37

The wind was cold, and Nico stopped walking to slide his jacket off his shoulders. He pulled Angel to a stop and held it up. "Put this on. It's cold."

She shook her head. "You'll freeze. Besides, I have a sweater."

"It's not enough," he insisted, slipping it up her arms and taking her hand.

He drew the sea air into his lungs as they continued along the craggy shoreline. He'd wanted to spend some time alone with her, away from the constant planning and anticipation of the fundraiser tomorrow night. The seaside town of Howth had been the perfect choice. Nestled on the outskirts of Dublin, it was small and green, the town winding its way down to a harbor filled with sailboats. He and Angel had stopped for lunch at a little inn, then walked past the harbor and along the wild coastline. Howth Lighthouse seemed to rise out of the sea in the distance, and farther out, one of the Martello towers that had been built along the Irish and English coastlines as a precaution against Napoleon at the end of the eighteenth century.

He looked down at Angel as they walked and was struck all over again by her loveliness. Her hair was long and loose, blowing around in the breeze, and her cheeks were pink from the cold. He was awash with love for her — love and lust and the desire to protect her from anything bad that might come knocking. He thought about his father, wondered if he'd felt the same powerful love for Nico's mother. What would he do in Nico's place? Would he have betrayed the Syndicate to keep her safe?

He felt sure the answer was yes. That kind of love trumped everything.

He pulled Angel's hand up under his arm to keep it warm as a gust of wind blew in off the water. She'd been quiet the past few days, but he was under no delusion that she was actually considering his offer to let him and Luca get the Darknet file alone. Something else was up, and he could only assume it had to do with the possibility of working with the FBI. They hadn't talked about it since the night he'd told her about his contact with Kane. He didn't want to pressure her, but once they had the file in hand, they would have to decide what to do with it: hand it over to Raneiro on their own or work with the FBI. And they would have less than a week to do it by Raneiro's deadline.

"I still feel bad about bringing Marco and Elia into this," Angel said.

"They've been apprised of the risks," Nico said. "Besides, having them here is just a precaution. We might not even need them."

After much discussion, he and Luca had decided to have Marco and Elia wait outside the gates of Sean Murdock's property. They would monitor the mic feed and watch the clock. If anyone went dark or something went wrong, Marco and Elia would come in after them. The added insurance was more about Angel than anything else. He could protect himself. So could Luca. But if someone tried to hurt Angel, he wanted every possible resource at his disposal. He would set the place on fire to get her out alive, but having two extra men couldn't hurt.

"I hope we don't," she said. "They're good men." She hesitated. "Will they be on the list of people with amnesty if we work with the FBI?"

Nico nodded. "And everyone else in the family."

He needed to call Kane. Find out if those were strings he could even pull. But there was no point doing it if Angel didn't want to work with the Feds. He still thought it was their best bet, and he felt sure Luca would agree. But he wouldn't do it without her blessing, too.

Her face was pensive as she gazed out over the water. "And you trust this agent? Kane?"

He thought about it, wanting to give her an honest answer. "I do. He fed me information that helped us find David in LA."

She looked up at him, surprise written on her face. "You didn't tell me."

"You were upset," he said, squeezing her hand. "I didn't want to give you something else to worry about. But it was Kane who found the wire transfer from Dante's aunt, and that was a big piece of the puzzle."

"What did you have to give him in return?" she asked.

"I gave up a former member of the family, a man who insisted on continuing a business we made clear was off limits." He didn't tell her the guy had been running a child pornography ring. He wouldn't bring anything ugly to her if it could be avoided.

"And that was enough?" she asked.

He nodded. "But this is different. This is big. Having their help makes bringing down Raneiro and disappearing when it's all over a lot more possible."

He saw the battle being waged inside her: revenge or possibility, the past or the future. He knew better than to think there was an easy answer.

## 38

"Close your eyes," Nico instructed. "Let your intuition tell you when to push, when to shimmy."

They were sitting at the dining room table, working on a lock attached to a doorknob Nico had removed from one of the bedrooms. She'd gotten used to the feel of the lock picking set in her hands, and she followed his instructions, keeping pressure on the tension wrench at the bottom of the lock with one hand and relaxing her hand around the pick in the other.

"Can you feel the pins?" Nico asked beyond the darkness behind her eyelids.

"Yes."

"Good. Now remember: you have to keep the torque on that wrench while you press up on the pick."

She'd been working with the set of lock picks for days, and she still couldn't always open the lock. When she did open it, she wasn't nearly fast enough. Basically, lock picking was not her forte. But it didn't matter. If Sean Murdock's study was locked, she would have to get it open somehow.

She refocused her attention on the mechanism inside the housing. There was slight give to the pins inside the lock as she pushed upward. The stubborn one — there almost always was one, according to Luca — was in the middle. She could feel its resistance, just a little bit greater than that of the others. She tried to see the different pieces in her mind, tried to match the sensory cues she was getting from the pick with her imagined visual of the lock.

A moment later she heard the soft click she'd come to associate with one of the pins being moved out of the way. It gave her confidence, and she continued with the remaining two pins. When she heard the last click, she opened her eyes and gave a little turn to the tension wrench. The knob turned freely.

"Nicely done," Nico said.

She exhaled. "I'm still too slow."

"That's okay," he said. "We don't even know if the door will be locked. If it is, just stay calm, close your eyes if you have to. You'll get it eventually."

"Eventually" wasn't very comforting, but there was nothing she could do about it. The fundraiser was tomorrow night. They were out of time. Luca was down at the local pub, preparing for the fundraiser in his own way. Nico and Angel had opted for a quiet night in. Tomorrow they would all be dressed to the nines, trying to steal something invaluable from Sean Murdock around all of his security and the dogs that were reported to be deadly.

He rubbed her back. "Why don't you go take a bath. I'll pour you a glass of wine."

She nodded. "I think I'll call David first. But I'll definitely take you up on that wine."

The words were out of her mouth before she had time to think about them. Could she have wine when she was pregnant? She thought she'd read somewhere that it was okay to have a little now and then.

She headed for the bedroom, thinking about the tiny life inside her. The life that was part of Nico, part of her. It made her feel more conflicted than ever. She needed to make a decision about the FBI. Needed to tell Nico so he could make the arrangements. But she still didn't know what to do.

She closed the bedroom door and picked up one of the phones, then dialed the house in Maine. The phone rang four times before Sara picked it up.

"Hello?"

"Hi, Sara, it's me."

"Hey! How are you?" Sara asked.

"I'm..." Angel sighed. "I'm good."

"Are you sure?" Sara asked, her voice shaded with concern.

"I'm just tired," Angel said. There was no point worrying Sara, or David, who would undoubtedly pick up on the fact that something was wrong.

"If you say so," Sara said. "I won't push, but if you need a friend, you know where to find me."

Angel smiled. "Thanks. How's David?"

"He's really, really good," Sara said.

"Yeah?"

"Yep. He's even gained a little weight."

Angel laughed. "Really?" She couldn't imagine it. He'd done nothing but pick at his food in the months since his abduction.

"Really. It looks good on him."

"And he's still taking his meds?" Angel asked.

"Like clockwork."

"That's great," Angel said. "You're a miracle worker."

"All the credit goes to David," Sara said. "He's really taken responsibility for getting well."

"I'm so happy to hear that."

She seemed to hesitate. "Are you guys getting close to being able to come home?"

"I think so," Angel said. "Another week or so."

It was the deadline Raneiro had given them. They would have to be done one way or another.

"That's great," Sara said. "David will be so happy to hear it. Do you want to talk to him?

"If it's not too much trouble."

"Not at all. He's down on the beach. Hold on."

She listened as Sara opened the doors off the living room and called to David. She could see it; the house in Maine settling into twilight, flames crackling in the fireplace, the sound of the waves crashing the beach below the house. Would she ever get back there? She hoped so. Or someplace like it, at least.

"Hi, Ange."

"Hi, loser."

"Someday that's going to stop being funny," he said.

"But not today," they said in unison.

She laughed. "I miss you like crazy."

"Me, too. Will you be home soon?"

"I think so. Another week or so," she said. "How are things there?"

He sighed, but it wasn't the tired sigh that had become so familiar. Instead it was filled with relief, with something too much like peace to be called anything else.

"They're good, Ange. *I'm* good."

"I'm so glad," she said, smiling.

He lowered his voice. "What's up, sis?"

"What do you mean? I'm just calling to say hi."

"Liar." He laughed. "It's me, remember? So what's up?"

She pulled at a loose thread on the old quilt covering the bed. "I don't know. I guess I'm just feeling... pensive."

"Sounds serious."

"It's not," she said. "I don't know. Maybe it is. I'm just... having a hard time putting the past behind me, I guess."

"Because you thought Nico was dead?"

"That might be part of it," she said. "And... I don't know. I was so sad and angry all that time he was gone, and now it's like I'm supposed to just forget about it because he's back."

"No one expects you to forget," David said. "I haven't forgotten what happened to me. Not like I could with this freak show of a hand I've got going on."

Her heart squeezed, but she didn't know if it was because it made her sad to be reminded that someone had hurt him or because it was the first time he'd been able to joke about it.

"So how do you do it then?" she asked. "How do you not forget and still manage to let it go?"

"I'm not sure I'm an expert," he said.

"You're doing it. That's all the expertise I need."

"I don't know, Ange. I was so tired. So fucking tired. By the time we got to Maine after those bastards came after us in Boston, I could hardly hold up my head. I thought it was the medication, but now I'm not so sure."

"What do you think it was now?" she asked softly.

"I think I was carrying too much shit around," he said. "All this... bitterness and rage about what happened to me. It seemed so unfair."

"It was unfair."

"Maybe. But life isn't always fair. We know that firsthand, and as shitty as that may be, I guess I finally figured out that I only have a finite amount of energy to spend, and it's kind of dumb to spend it being pissed about something I can't change."

"What if you could change it?" she asked.

"I can't. And neither can you," he insisted. "You might think you can, but whatever you do from here on out will only be to make yourself feel better. Except it won't actually make you feel better, and it won't change anything either."

"Maybe." She said it, but she wasn't sure. She didn't want to let go of her belief that seeing Raneiro dead would somehow level the playing field, give her back everything she'd lost.

"There's no maybe about it," he said. "Do you want to spend your life looking back? Or do you want to build something new?"

She didn't say anything for a long moment, his words ringing in her ears. Finally she sighed. "Is that a rhetorical question?"

He laughed. "Not really."

"Let me get back to you then."

"It's a deal. But Ange?"

"Yeah?"

"I want to build something new. It would be really cool if you were there with me."

She smiled into the phone. "Love you, dork."

"That's a new one." She could hear the smile in his voice. "I love you, too."

She hung up and set the phone on the bed. Then she put her hands over her still-flat stomach, imagining the new life beginning to form inside her.

*Do you want to spend your life looking back? Or do you want to build something new?*

## 39

"How long do you want us to give you?" Marco asked the next night. He was every bit as gargantuan as she remembered, his gray eyes as cold as the wind in Maine.

He and Elia had arrived early that morning. They'd greeted Angel warmly, and she'd hugged them for all she was worth. She hadn't realized how much she missed them, or how much she'd grown accustomed to seeing them on a daily basis in Boston.

Nico and Luca spent the day filling them in and doing checks on all the equipment while Angel practiced with the lock picking set. She didn't get much faster, but by the end of the day, she'd gotten more consistent. It was something.

Now they were in the dining room, going over everything one more time. Angel was already dressed, the green gown gown hugging her curves under the lace, showing just enough cleavage to be suggestive without being outright sexy. The CWI fundraiser was a high dollar event. She needed to fit in with the A-List that would include socialites and philanthropists, politicians and business people, and she'd swept up her hair with tiny rhinestone pins that glimmered when the light caught them.

"Give us until midnight unless I tell you otherwise," Nico said. "Murdock isn't going to deal with us while he has a houseful of guests, even if we get caught. But if we're not out when the other guests start to leave, consider it a call for the calvary."

Elia folded his enormous biceps over his chest. His shaved head made him look menacing, and she had to remind herself that he *was* menacing for anyone who crossed him. Who crossed them.

"And the mics will be live the whole time?"

Nico nodded. "If they go silent, it's a sign something's wrong."

Marco leveled his gaze at Angel, already dressed for the fundraiser. "You sure you want in on this?"

"I've been offered more than one chance to bow out." She smiled. "I'm good."

"Well, we can be inside Murdock's compound inside of five minutes. Say the word and we're there."

She laughed. "Have you even seen Murdock's compound?"

"Not in person," Marco said. "But it doesn't matter. Anyone messes with you, we come in shooting. And when we come in shooting, we can get anywhere inside of five minutes."

The thought should have put her at ease, but all she could think about was how much she cared about these men. How much she loved each of them. She didn't want them to risk their lives for her anymore.

She stood on tiptoe and kissed his cheek. "Thank you. But this is going to be easy. In and out."

They loaded the gear into the van they'd rented, and she watched as they strapped on the kevlar sent by Farrell Black. She eyed Nico's tux. The stakes were higher than ever. She needed him to come out of this alive.

"You are putting one of those on, aren't you?" she asked him.

He undid one of his buttons and gave her a glimpse of the black vest underneath his dress shirt. "I'd put one on you if I could get away with it under that dress."

She thought about the baby — their baby — and suddenly wanted to call the whole thing off. To run as far away as they could get before Raneiro's deadline. But that was her fear talking, and no good decision was ever made out of fear. There was no way around this; they could only get through it to come out the other side.

Nico and Luca clipped the tiny mics to their suit jackets. Then Nico slipped one inside the bodice of her dress, his fingers sending a current of electricity through her body as they brushed her breasts. He kept his eyes on hers while he clipped the device where it couldn't be seen, then touched his lips to her cheek.

"Call me if you need me."

She nodded, and they inserted the tiny wireless earpieces that would allow them to hear each other. She pulled a loose piece of hair a bit lower to hide hers, then looked at Nico and Luca.

"Won't someone see your earpieces?"

"Probably not," Nico said. "They're pretty small. But even if someone does, it's no big deal. We won't be the only one with them at this event."

Angel understood. The guest list comprised of some of the most powerful people in the world. Personal security would be evident, and security meant communication.

They did another mic check to make sure Marco and Elia could read them now that they were attached, and to make sure they could hear each other. Then the two men were driving off in the van, wanting to get in place outside the Murdock property before it got too congested with traffic.

A few minutes later, a limo pulled into the driveway. Nico held open the door for Angel.

"You really know how to treat a lady, Mr. Vitale," she said, sliding into the back.

"Only the best for you," he said. "Although I'd prefer my own car to this rental."

She laughed. "Don't be a snob."

Luca sat across from them, then turned around to confirm their destination with the gray haired driver. Angel took advantage of the opportunity to take Nico's hand.

"I've been thinking about what you said."

"I've said a lot of things."

"About how it might come down to life or revenge," she said. "And?"

She drew in a breath. "And I want life. With you."

"Are you saying what I think you're saying?" he asked.

She nodded. "If you think we should work with the Feds, let's do it." She hesitated, thinking about all the dirt she'd gathered on the

Syndicate in the months when she thought Nico was dead. All the information she'd planned to use to make them pay. "I might even be able to up the ante for your friend, Kane."

Luca turned around to face them, and the car rolled forward down the driveway. Nico squeezed her hand, bent over to kiss her softly on the lips. This was it. The beginning of the end, and hopefully the beginning of their freedom.

She pushed away her regret that Raneiro wouldn't pay for his crimes the way she wanted him to. Some things were more important than revenge. She repeated it in her head until she believed it.

# 40

Luca handed their invitations to the driver as they joined the line of cars approaching the big iron gate. The line was full of limos, Towncars, and Mercedes, as well as a host of high-end European sports cars. Their taillights lit up the night in a wash of red, and Nico felt a sudden rush of fear, as if it was some kind of foreshadowing for the night ahead. He glanced over at Angel, her graceful neck exposed by the sweep of her hair, breasts swelling under the bodice of her gown. She belonged to him, and he would do anything to protect her.

Anything.

Finally it was their turn at the gate. The driver handed over the invitation, and they were ushered onto the long drive leading to the Murdock mansion. Lights lit up the driveway, the house a glittering jewel on the other side of a long stretch of the lawn.

They waited behind the cars waiting to deposit their passengers at the front of the house. When they reached the valet, their driver got out of the car and came around to let them out. Luca stepped from the car first, giving his hand to Angel. Nico emerged last. He was glad the event was private. There had been a firestorm of activity after his press release, and he wasn't ready to face the media attention. If everything went according to plan, he'd never have to face it; he and Angel would work with Kane and the Feds to set up a meeting with Raneiro, then hand everything over to them and be on their way. He touched a possessive hand to the small of her back as they made their way up the wide stone steps to the carved double doors. She had agreed to do it his way. They would get their new beginning.

They just had to get through the next week.

They entered a soaring foyer, a massive, glittering chandelier lighting the space from above. The floors were marble, the walls framed with mahogany wainscoting and elaborate moldings. A double staircase curved upward to the second floor — the location of Sean Murdock's study.

"See you on the flip side," Luca murmured, grabbing a glass of champagne from a passing waiter and slipping into the crowd so he could case the place.

Nico was aware of the murmur of interest, the curious glances of the other guests. He avoided their gazes and tucked Angel's hand into his arm, then followed the crowd to an expansive ballroom at the center of the house.

A small orchestra played in one corner, and the center of the gleaming parquet floor was cleared for dancing. Couples were already waltzing there, the women's gowns fluttering in a lush wash of color that stood in contrast to the stark black and white tuxedoes worn by the men.

He took two glasses of champagne off a passing tray, handed one to Angel, and touched his glass to hers. "To life." He looked into her eyes, as deep and green as the rarest emerald. "And new beginnings."

She smiled. "Life. And new beginnings."

They drank, and Nico let his eyes roam the room, careful to keep his expression casual, almost bored. There were four guards in the ballroom, all of them in tuxes designed to help them blend in. Nico wasn't fooled. Their watchful eyes gave them away, as did the occasional movement of their mouths — obviously talking into hidden mics — when no one was nearby.

"Let's take a walk," he said to Angel.

They moved out of the ballroom and were stopped by Morgan VanPelt, CEO of one of MediaComm's biggest competitors. Nico nodded and smiled, offered terse explanations for the "confusion" surrounding reports of his death, and moved on as quickly as possible. It was't the first time they were waylaid by gossip mongers disguised as well wishers, but Nico made it a point to be friendly — if not forthcoming — in an effort to stay as below the radar as possible.

Their halfhearted attempts at socializing gave them the benefit of seeing the house, getting a handle on the layout and the position of the guards. Some of them were floaters, but others were relatively stationary, giving Nico a chance to get a somewhat reliable count. By the time they made their way through the grand hall, the living room, parlors and media room, the bar and recreational room (complete with four billiard tables and another bar), Nico had counted four guards in the big room, two in the smaller ones, and approximately ten roving the party from one room to the next. And then there was Ian Hayes, who seemed to be everywhere, watching Nico with careful eyes. The stationary guards weren't a problem, but they would need to keep an eye on the rovers — and especially on Ian.

They were making their way back to the ballroom when a voice stopped him from his right.

"Nico Vitale."

He turned to find Sean Murdock eyeing him with a mixture of interest and suspicion.

Nico knew the feeling.

Ian stood near the wall behind Sean, arms folded in front of his body. Nico was surprised to find the man's gaze not on him but on Angel, his eyes hungrily roaming her body. He tensed, fighting the urge to strangle the man into unconsciousness.

"Sean." Nico held out his hand. "Nice to finally meet you in person. I'm a big fan of your work."

He was smaller than he appeared in the photos Nico had seen online and on the news. Everything about his appearance was unremarkable — from his slight frame to his wire glasses to the brown hair the was one step away from receding. Everything except his eyes, which were intelligent and piercing. Nico knew immediately that it would be a mistake to underestimate the software genius.

He might be a brainiac — but he was a dangerous one.

Sean shook his hand. "That's nice of you to say. I was surprised to get the call from your assistant given your recent... reintroduction to society."

Nico smiled. "I've been away too long. Have to get back in the game."

Sean nodded. "Things change quickly in this day and age. Simply being present is an advantage."

"That's very true," Nico said, trying to read between the lines.

Nico thought back to the men who had broken into the flat in Rome. Had they asked for his name? He couldn't remember, but he didn't think so. They'd been more concerned with what he and Angel were doing talking to McDermott, and his mention of Raneiro had effectively deflected the attention from him to Donati.

Still, he couldn't assume Sean didn't know he had been the one questioning Desmond McDermott in Rome. And it didn't matter anyway. Sean could watch him all night. In fact, Nico preferred it. All the better for Angel to sneak upstairs.

Sean turned his attention on Angel. "And who is your lovely friend?"

Unlike Ian, his gaze was purely intellectual, as if Angel was a mathematical problem that could be worked by following a simple formula.

"Sean Murdock, Angelica Bondesan." He used Angel's old name on purpose, hoping to throw off Sean — and Ian, who was still looking at her like a jackal about to eat her whole — at least temporarily. They might already know who she was, but there was no reason to hand them the knowledge.

Sean kissed the top of Angel's hand. It was bland, almost effeminate, and Nico wondered suddenly if Sean were gay.

"Lovely to meet you," Sean said.

Angel tipped her head. "The pleasure is mine."

Sean straightened. "Well, I'm so glad you could attend. Clean water is one of the most important problems facing the world, don't you agree?"

"Absolutely," Nico said. "I've made an additional donation to the foundation. I hope you'll find it helpful."

"That's very kind. I'm sure we'll be seeing each other again."

Nico was still trying to figure out if there was any hidden meaning in the words when Sean turned from the room, Ian Hayes on his heels. Maybe they'd get lucky and Ian would follow Sean around like a puppy dog all night. That would be convenient.

He waited until they were well out of earshot to murmur in Angel's ear. "It's late. Let's get moving."

## 41

The conversation with Sean had thrown her. She'd noticed Ian Hayes undressing her with his eyes, but it was Sean who made her skin crawl. His eyes were cold — almost reptilian. Every instinct in her body screamed danger. It didn't make sense. He was at least six inches shorter than Nico, and a good fifty pounds lighter.

But she couldn't help it. something about the man gave her the creeps.

She and Nico were making their way back to the ballroom when Luca's voice sounded in her earpiece. "I count eight rovers."

Nico turned his head. "Negative. There are ten."

"You're the boss," Luca said. "I've got eyes on three."

Nico looked around the room, and Angel saw the shrewdness in his gaze, knew he was counting. "I've got two here."

"Good enough to move?" Luca asked.

Nico's gaze flickered to Angel. "As good as it's going to get. I'm sending her now."

"Copy that."

He looked down at her. "You sure about this?" he murmured.

"I'm sure," she said. "Look around."

He did, and she knew he saw the curiosity leveled at him from all sides of the room. He would be a gossip magnet for awhile yet, and while it had been the price of admission to the fundraiser, it also meant he wouldn't be able to operate unnoticed in a room full of his peers.

He sighed. "Be careful. Be fast. And say the word if you need me."

"Will do." She wanted to kiss him, but she didn't want to draw attention to herself, so she slipped into the crowd and headed for the grand hall.

She turned away from the foyer and headed for the kitchen. The house was old — even older than the Boston brownstone. Big, old houses usually had staircases at the back, leading straight from the kitchen to the upper floors. They were a throwback to another time. Back then, the dirty work of kitchens and laundry and servants was considered unseemly, hidden from the eyes of guests and even, to some degree, from the owners of the houses themselves. The servant's staircase allowed for the ferrying of food, drinks, and other supplies to the upper floors without forcing polite company to acknowledge their existence. It was disgusting to think about now, but it had been a different time, and she was grateful for it as she wound her way through the boiling pots and white-coated staff in the kitchen at the back of the house. She was obviously a guest, and since no one knew who she was or how important, she was allowed to pass without question.

She scanned the space quickly and found what she was looking for near the butler's pantry. The door was narrow, its threshold low. She looked both ways and put her hand on the knob, praying it was still in use. Picking a lock in a deserted hallway on the second floor was one thing; trying to do it when the kitchen staff could come upon her at any moment was another.

She breathed a sigh of relief when the knob turned easily in her hand. A moment later she was slipping into a tiny vestibule so dark she couldn't see her own hand in front of her face. Fighting panic, she leaned against the door and opened her evening bag, digging around until her fingers closed around the tiny flashlight she'd brought in case she needed it in Sean's study. She twisted the top and the staircase was illuminated in front of her.

It was low-ceilinged and narrow, with one staircase winding upward and one winding down, probably into a cellar. She moved upward, trying not to think about what she would find in the other direction.

The staircase wound around two landings before she found a door. She put her ear to the wood, listening for voices. When she didn't hear anything, she took a deep breath and stepped into the hall. It was wide, lit with sconces every few feet, the floor lined with richly patterned carpets that looked to be very old.

She was obviously in the master's wing of the manor house now.

She called to mind the blueprint she'd memorized of the second floor, marking the doors down either side of the hall until her eyes came to the one that should be Sean Murdock's study.

Now or never.

She made her way toward it, praying it wasn't locked. The hall was deserted, the sounds of the party below muffled through the thick walls and carpets. But her isolation only served to make her more aware that she was trespassing. That if she were discovered, it would be difficult to concoct an excuse for being on the second floor when it was so obviously off limits to guests.

She stooped at the door and turned the knob, cursing quietly when it didn't move.

Locked.

Fuck.

She had been hoping to avoid using the lock picks, but there was no way around it. She pulled the set out of her bag and went to work, inserting the tension wrench at the bottom and slipping the pick into the top the way she'd practiced, raking the pins, feeling for the resistance that would guide her hand.

She tried to keep up the torque on the wrench while she pushed upward on the pick, but it wasn't an easy balance to strike, and the wrench slipped from her hand and fell to the floor.

She bent down to pick it up, then tightened one of the pins in her hair when a piece of hair fell forward into her eyes. Damn. She had too much exposure out here in the hall. She needed to get inside the study where she stood a chance at remaining undetected.

She went back to work with the wrench and pick, forcing herself to take her time, to feel the pins hidden from view, even though she wanted nothing more than to rattle the knob in frustration.

Time seemed to stop. She had no idea how many minutes passed before she finally felt the first pin move. She closed her eyes, breathing slowly while she felt for the remaining pins. She manipulated them one by one, working her way farther into the lockset, getting them out of the way one at a time until she heard the soft click of the last one.

She turned the wrench and the door opened.

She breathed a sigh of relief, put the tools back in her bag, and slipped inside the room.

## 42

She stood near the door and scanned the darkened room. It was a big space, with plenty of room for the wall to wall bookshelves, sofa and love seat, antique carved desk, wing chairs, and liquor cabinet, plus several small tables. When her eyes had adjusted to the darkness, she crossed to the desk.

There was a leather blotter and a cup with pens, scissors, and a letter opener, but no computer. She opened the drawers, rifling through paperclips and receipts, phone chargers and computer cables. She even found an external hard drive in the top drawer.

But no computer.

She looked around the room, weighing her options. After a brief hesitation, she held onto the hard drive and started searching the rest of the study. Fifteen minutes later, panic was getting the best of her. Unless she was missing it, there was no computer in Sean Murdock's study. She'd checked the desk twice, the bookshelves, the liquor cabinet, even the end tables around the sofa.

Shit.

"There's no computer in here," she said, knowing the mic would pick it up.

"Nothing?" Luca's voice.

"An external hard drive," she said. "But no way to check and see what's on it."

"Think you can get to Murdock's bedroom?" Luca asked. "That's the next most likely place for his computer."

"Negative." Nico. "Hayes just walked up the stairs. Get out of there."

Her blood turned cold as she thought about the lascivious stare of the Murdock's head of security. It had been almost punishing, like looking at her made him angry and he couldn't wait to take it out on her.

"What about the file?" she asked.

"Take the hard drive," Nico said. "And get out of there."

"Copy." She stuffed the hard drive in her bag, frustration threatening to overtake her. She'd finally decided to put the past behind her and their ticket to freedom was nowhere to be found.

"Keep an eye out for…"

But the rest of his words were lost as the door to the study swung open. Ian Hayes stood in the doorway, backlit by the lights from the hall.

"Well, well, well," he said. "Doing a little exploring?"

"I was looking for a phone actually," she said. "Mine's dead, and it's so noisy downstairs."

The lie rolled smoothly off her tongue. She would have been proud of herself if there had been any sign it was going to do her any good.

Hayes shut the door with an ominous click and advanced into the dark room. She forced herself not to back up, not to look scared or guilty, as she clutched her bag — and the hard drive inside of it — close to her body. Whatever happened, she had to get it out of the compound.

"Why am I finding it hard to believe you came up here just for a phone?" Hayes said, running a hand absent-mindedly along the back of the sofa as he came closer to her position in front of the desk.

She smiled. "Probably because no modern girl would let her cell phone die at the hottest party of the year."

"Or maybe because you're here with Vitale," he said, still advancing. "And because you were in Rome, nosing around McDermott."

She didn't bother lying. "That was a favor for Raneiro Donati."

She knew immediately that the name wouldn't have the same effect with Hayes that it had with Murdock's men in Rome. He just smiled, like he was bored, and kept walking until his body was up against hers, her ass pressed against the edge of Sean Murdock's desk.

"The funny thing is I almost didn't come in here." He held up something in front of her face. "Then I saw this."

It was her hairpin, and she remembered dropping the tension wrench, bending down to pick it up, the piece of loose hair she'd secured — obviously with one of the other pins.

She shrugged. "Sucks being a girl sometimes."

The feel of his erection through his trousers gave her a flashback to Dante and the time he had almost assaulted her in the basement of Nico's headquarters. That it sucked being a girl sometimes was the understatement of the century, and she could only hope Nico and Luca were picking up the conversation and had a plan for getting her out of there before Marco and Elia stormed the house.

His eyes dropped to her breasts, and she took advantage of the opportunity to look for something she could use as a weapon. The desk lamp was out of reach, but she might be able to get to the letter opener. It would be messy though, counter to their plan to get in and out with no one the wiser until Murdock found the Darknet file missing.

She cringed as Hayes slid a hand up her thigh, his palm cold and clammy against her bare skin. She pushed at his chest, but he just moved in closer, pulling up her dress, wedging himself between her thighs.

"You really don't want to do this," she said.

He ground his hard-on into her, and she felt bile rise in her throat. No one was allowed to touch her like this but Nico.

No one.

She turned her head, reached for the letter opener. Hayes's hand had found its way to the cleft between her legs, and she went cold as he pulled her panties aside. The letter opened was almost in her hand. Almost...

She was preparing herself for the assault of his fingers, imagining how good it would feel to sink the letter opener into the bastard's belly, when he suddenly disappeared from in front of her. It took her a few seconds to orient herself, to realize he was now on the floor, a beast of a man hunched over him, punching him in the face again and again.

Nico.

"Motherfucker," he muttered, Hayes's bones crouching under the force of the blows.

She was frozen, still clutching the bag holding the hard drive in one hand, and improbably, the letter opener in the other. When had she gotten her hand around it? She thought vaguely that Nico might kill the man turning bloody under his fists, but then someone else was there, pulling Nico off the ruined face that belonged to Hayes.

"We need to get out of here," Luca said to him. "Okay?"

Nico was breathing hard, his eyes glazed over, but he nodded. He turned to Angel, gently smoothing her dress before taking her in his arms.

"Are you okay?"

"I'm fine," she said. She was dimly aware that she might not be fine later, but they needed to get the hard drive out of Murdock's house before someone realized Hayes was missing.

"You guys got her?" It was Elia's voice in her headset.

"Confirmed," Luca said.

He bent to Hayes's body, felt for a pulse, then pulled something from the unconscious man's ear. "He's alive, and he disconnected his mic, probably to keep the other guards from hearing what he was about to do." Rape her. That's what Luca meant — what Hayes had been about to do. "That buys us some time."

Nico took her hand. "Let's get out of here."

"Do you have the hard drive?" Luca asked.

She nodded, clutching the bag harder to keep from shaking. "Let's go."

Luca checked the hallway before giving them the signal that it was clear. Then they were out of the study, closing the door behind them and heading for the staircase. They emerged into the busy kitchen and moved calmly through the throng of cooks and servers, all of them acting like they had every business being there.

They emerged into the grand hall and threaded their way through the thinning crowd. It was late, and some of the guests had already started to leave. They were almost to the door when someone spoke loudly behind them.

"Leaving us so soon?"

They stopped, turned around. Sean Murdock stood near the stairs, his expression unreadable. She saw Nico's hand shift toward his waist, knew he'd draw his gun if it came to it, even though they'd planned to avoid it to protect the party guests.

"I'm afraid so," Nico said. "But it's been...enlightening. I had no idea your interests were so varied."

Sean smiled, and in the pause that followed, Angel prepared to get out of the way. If Nico drew his gun, chaos would ensue. Luca would be right behind him, and it would only be a matter of moments before Marco and Elia appeared to assist. They were better off not having to worry about her.

"Well," Sean finally said. "It's important to give back, don't you think?"

Nico didn't say anything right away, and Angel was painfully aware of the passing seconds. They needed to get off the property and into the van with Marco and Elia before someone figured out Ian Hayes was missing.

Nico's jaw twitched, and she knew he was reigning in his temper. Sean was the worst kind of liar. One who hid behind good deeds that would never be enough to make up for the misery he brought to the world.

"Absolutely," Nico said. "In fact, it's something I'm putting a lot of thought into these days. You're quite the inspiration."

Sean opened his arms. "Just doing my part."

"Good luck with that," Luca said.

And then they were out the door, heading past the valet and toward the gates.

# 43

Nico put his arms around Angel as soon as they were inside the van. "Are you sure you're okay?"

She nodded, and he grabbed a blanket that was folded on the floor and put it around her shoulders. He looked into her eyes, and the shock and fear there made him want to turn around, tear Sean Murdock and every one of his men apart.

"I will never let anyone hurt you," he told her. "Never. Okay?" She nodded. "Okay."

"Where's the hard drive?" Luca asked gently.

Angel opened her bag, pulled out the small blue device and handed it to him. "I don't know what's on it," she said. "There was no computer."

Marco climbed into the back while Elia sped toward the airport. He opened a laptop and connected the hard drive from Sean's office.

"What am I looking for?" he asked.

"Something called Darknet," Nico said.

"Hold on." Marco tapped at the keys.

Nico glanced at Elia in the driver's seat, his face illuminated by the lights on the dash. "How are we doing?" Nico asked him.

Elia checked the rearview mirror. "So far, so good."

Nico knew firsthand how influential well placed bribes could be. Dublin was Sean's territory. None of them would rest easy until they were out of the country.

Marco handed him the laptop. "This what you're looking for?"

Nico looked at the dates and names on the screen, then continued to a seemingly endless list of weaponry, from handguns to automatics, grenades to RPGs. Next to each entry was a quantity and numbers that looked like coordinates. The location of the weapons cache in question, Nico guessed.

"This is exactly what we're looking for," he said, his eyes still on the screen.

"That's some heavy shit, boss."

Nico nodded. "It is indeed some heavy shit."

Raneiro had been right; Sean Murdock was much more — or less — than a software genius. He'd been brokering weapons deals to some of the most savage warlords around the world — people Nico had seen on the news raping and pillaging, preventing countries in turmoil from establishing law and order and honest governments. They were power hungry thugs with access to weaponry usually reserved for countries with military budgets in the billions. Sean Murdock had made it all accessible to anybody with enough cash, and from the names on the list, it was cash that had been accumulated drug running and trafficking. He wondered how many of the people on the list had benefactors within the governments of first world countries. It was information that could change the face of law and order all over the world, that could free people from fear of death at the hands of tyrants, that could stabilize countries in the midst of civil wars.

He'd been fooling himself to think there was a clean way of conducting his business. Had been rationalizing by telling himself he was mitigating the damage. Maybe he hadn't sanctioned weapons sales to vicious killers the way Sean Murdock had done, but Nico had done his share of illegal things. Picking and choosing which income streams were palatable was just a way to justify how he'd made his living. How his father had made a living. These were the kinds of people in the world of the Syndicate — the world he'd been part of.

People like Sean Murdock. Like Raneiro Donati.

He looked over at Angel, her face turned to the window. She was the only pure thing in his life, and he suddenly wanted nothing more than to be worthy of her. To spend his life proving he was a good enough man to stand by her side. He'd almost destroyed them both.

Now it was time to make it right.

# 44

Angel understood why Nico trusted Braden Kane the moment he walked into the hotel room in Monaco. He was tall and broad shouldered — so muscular he could have held his own with any of Nico's men. But it was his eyes that got Angel's attention. They were warm and green, the color of moss. Angel knew instinctively that he was a good man.

"You ready for this?" he asked Nico.

Nico nodded. "Raneiro's deadline is the day after tomorrow. I don't want to risk setting it up too late."

"We'll do our due diligence by tracing his location, but if all goes according to plan, it won't matter; we'll take him into custody once he's incriminated himself with the Darknet file," Kane said.

"Do you have the agreement?" Nico asked him.

Kane withdrew a folded set of papers from his pocket and handed them to Nico. "It's all there. Amnesty for your people, per your request, and a promise that we'll only seek to prosecute the people at the top of the Syndicate." He shook his head. "It wasn't easy."

Nico nodded. "I appreciate it." He tipped his head to the papers in his hand. "Mind if I take a look?"

"Not at all."

Angel walked to the balcony door and looked out over the Mediterranean while Nico unfolded the papers. They'd chosen Monte Carlo for its proximity to Rome, almost certainly Raneiro's choice of meeting places, and its relative quiet. Luca had moved on, his location undisclosed, as had Marco and Elia. They'd parted ways at the Dublin airport, and Angel had been overcome with a feeling of loss. Would she ever see them again? Would they be okay?

She hoped so. They deserved a new beginning, too.

"How are you holding up?"

She turned to find Kane standing next to her, studying her with his forest green eyes. "I'm okay. Ready to have this over with."

He nodded. "You've been through a lot."

"And you're sure you'll be able to get my brother out of Maine?" she asked.

She'd checked in with David when they arrived in Monaco, and while she hadn't been able to give him details, he knew they were going to have to leave the country. She'd been surprised by his response.

"I think I'm ready for a change of scenery anyway, Ange."

It had made her smile. He sounded like his old self, and she was actually starting to believe they might really have another chance to begin again.

"We'll get him out," Kane said. "Nico definitely made it easier for us by keeping him on the island."

The island. Another thing that would probably be lost to them forever. Then again, she was starting to learn there was nothing new without the shedding of something old. Maybe that's how it was supposed to be. You could only carry so much before it got difficult to move forward at all.

"Just be careful with him," she said. "he's been through a lot, too."

"You have my word." He hesitated. "You know where you want to go yet?"

She smiled. "We have an idea."

He nodded.

"Looks good," Nico said behind them. They turned around to face him. "Where do I sign?"

Kane crossed the room and pointed to the line at the bottom of the agreement and its matching copy. When it was all done, he pocketed one and handed one to Nico. Then he held out his hand. Nico shook it.

"Let's do this, partner," Kane said.

He picked up a Tracphone, then attached headphones to it. He handed one of the earbuds to Angel and put one in his own ear. Nico met Angel's eyes, then dialed. Angel listened to the phone ring in Rome.

"Who is this?" a smooth voice asked on the other end of the phone.

"It's me," Nico said. "I have what you asked for."

"So I heard," Raneiro said. "Apparently you made quite an impression in Dublin."

"I did what was necessary to secure the file, per your request. Now I want your assurance that we'll walk — me, Angelica Rossi, her brother, and anyone else who works for me that wants out."

Kane met her eyes. Nico was going through the motions, asking the questions Raneiro would expect him to ask if he was concerned about securing his freedom. If he weren't working with the FBI.

"Of course," Raneiro said. "We had a deal."

"How do I know you'll honor it?" Nico asked.

"I suppose you'll simply have to trust me."

"You haven't made that easy to do," Nico said.

"Be that as it may, I don't see that you have a choice."

Nico hesitated. "Fine. When and where?"

"Let's stay on schedule and call it the day after tomorrow at eleven PM," he said. "The dock we use for shipments in Rome. You remember the one?"

"I do," Nico said.

"Fine. I'll see you then. And Nico?"

"Yes?"

"Bring the girl."

"That wasn't part of the deal," Nico said.

"It is now."

"Not if I say it isn't."

"I"m afraid you're overestimating your bargaining power," Raneiro said.

"Why?" Nico asked. "She has nothing to do with this. I have what you want."

There was a pause on the other end of the phone. "I will admit that you have reason to distrust me. But I also have reason to be nervous. How do I know you don't plan to kill me?"

"If I want to kill you, having Angelica Rossi there won't stop me."

"Perhaps. But you are nothing if not a gentleman, Nico. And no gentleman wants the woman he loves caught in the crossfire, especially when it's already happened once before."

"How do I know you won't hurt her?" Nico asked. "You're only making our trust issues more complicated."

Raneiro chuckled, and a chill ran up Angel's spine. "It's too late to hope that our relationship will be simple. Bring the girl and the file. Otherwise you're both dead."

# 45

"Are you worried?" she asked Nico the next night as they walked along the path that ran parallel to the water in Monte Carlo. They'd eaten at a little place with outdoor tables, the lights of the harbor reflecting off the water as waves rolled gently toward land. Tomorrow they would fly to Rome and meet up with Kane and the FBI, but tonight had been just for them.

Nico pulled her closer as they walked. "I'm worried about you."

"I'll be fine," she said.

"That's what you always say."

"And it's always been true."

He kissed her head, and she was glad he didn't call her on the lie. She leaned her head on his shoulder. She'd had one glass of champagne at dinner, not wanting Nico to be suspicious if she refused. She'd almost told him about the baby more than once, but she knew the time wasn't right. It would be selfish, a way to share the responsibility of the knowledge. Nico needed to focus on the meeting with Raneiro. On getting out alive. He couldn't afford to be distracted. Besides, she had to go with him now; Raneiro had demanded her presence.

They stopped under a light near the water and leaned against the railing. The wind was chilly coming in off the water, and Nico tightened his hold on her. His shirt brushed against her skin, and she felt the ripple of his solid chest as he pulled her closer. Her body answered the call of his, heat already building between her legs as he lowered his mouth to hers. The kiss was gentle at first, but it didn't take long to grow deeper, and he slanted his mouth over hers, his tongue greedily invading her mouth as she met him stroke for stroke. She shivered when he pulled away.

"You're cold," he said. "Let's get back to the hotel."

"That's not why I shivered," she said, pressing her body against his. "But yes. Let's get back to the hotel."

Ten minutes later they burst into their room, their hands roaming each other's body before the door was even fully closed. Nico pushed her against the wall next to the door and slipped off her sweater, then pulled down the top of her dress to expose her bare breasts. He cupped them in his hands, closing his mouth around one of the pink nipples. Her breasts were even more sensitive than usual, and she almost cried out from the pleasure-pain of it.

She arched her back, pressing the flesh farther into his mouth. He groaned in response, and a rush of wetness soaked her panties as she felt his erection strain against her stomach. He tongued the pink peak of her nipple, then sucked until she gasped, lifting a leg up around his hip so she could press her aching pussy against the rigid line of his cock.

He reached down with one hand, grabbing her ass, pressing her more fully against him until he was nestled between her thighs good and tight.

She slipped her hand between them, rubbed her palm over his cock, felt it pulse under her hand. She was undoing his belt, dying to feel the satiny length of him in her hand, when he tugged the dress lower on her body. It fell to the floor, and he knelt at her feet, lifting one of her legs onto his shoulder.

She leaned her head back against the wall, dizzy with desire as he kissed his way up her thigh, nibbling at the pale, tender skin right near her pussy. Reaching down, she slid her fingers into his thick hair and pulled, wanting his mouth on her.

She thought he might tease her in response, might make her wait. Instead he pushed aside her panties and spread her open with his tongue, lapping at the petals of her sex, burying his face in her like he couldn't get enough.

She clutched his hair tighter. "Nico…"

He flicked his tongue over her clit, then covered it with his mouth and sucked as he slid his fingers inside her. She moved her hips in time with the motion of his fingers, reaching for the climax that was already there like a promise. She almost reached it when he pulled out his fingers. She balled up her fists, but she didn't have time to focus on her frustration. A moment later, he spread her wide open with with his hands, exposing every inch of her.

"God, you're beautiful, Angel."

He licked her exposed clit, and she shuddered at the torture of it, his mouth working every crease, every crevice. He slid his mouth down to her opening, fucking her with his tongue while he fingered her clit, moving in circles until she was pressing into his face, beyond inhibition, beyond anything but the orgasm she needed like air.

"I'm going to come, Nico. I'm going to come so hard."

"Hm-hmm," he said against her clit, the vibration of his voice adding another element of bliss to the motion of his fingers moving in and out of her, the intense, almost unbearable ecstasy of his tongue lapping at her clit.

She ground her hips against his mouth, rushing for the top of the mountain, racing for it, desperate to reach the top. He moved his fingers faster, sucked harder, and then she was tipping off the edge, free falling into a void of pleasure where nothing existed but the explosion at the center of her body.

She was still coming back to reality when he stood between her legs. She unzipped his pants while he kissed her hard and deep, her pleasure a sweet tang on his tongue. Then he was in her hand — long, hard, and heavy.

Ready for her.

She stroked him, felt the drop of cum at the tip of his cock, massaged it around his tip.

"I need to be inside of you, Angel." He buried his face in her neck, and she heard all of her own desperation in his voice. "Let me get a condom."

She stopped him from leaving, looked into his eyes. "Don't.'

He held her gaze, his cock pulsing in her hand. "Are you sure?"

"I'm sure."

She wrapped a leg around one of his hips and he lifted her up, braced her against the wall until both feet were off the ground. She guided him to her opening, relishing the moment when he stood poised on the threshold of their mutual desire. Then he was driving into her, pressing her against the wall as he thrust, dragging slowly out of her, then thrusting again, the friction against her clit sending shockwaves of pleasure so intense she had to force herself not to come too soon, to wait so they could come together.

He was like a wild animal, mindless, clutching her ass, pounding her pussy into oblivion as she held on, feeling his desperation. Then he was moving faster, his breath shallow, and she knew he was close. She let go, allowed herself to climb, to fall all the way onto him when he pushed into her, letting him hit the top of her womb until it hurt so good she felt tears of pleasure sting her eyes.

"Come inside me, baby," she coaxed. "Spill it into me."

The words pushed him over the edge, and he growled as he drove ferociously into her, shuddering as he poured his come into her pussy, the heat of it causing a wave of pleasure to push her the rest of the way. Then she was coming too, crying out as she shook against him, his strong arms holding her up until the last tremors had shaken her body.

He lifted her up, and she wrapped her legs around his waist.

"You're mine." It was as much a promise to her as a warning to anyone else, and he held her tight as he carried her to bed. "Always and forever, Angel. Mine."

# 46

Nico wasn't even surprised to find that it was raining in Rome, and he tried to avoid the gloom that settled over him as he and Angel made their way to the hotel where they would gear up for the meeting with Raneiro later that night. It was just rain. There was no such thing as a bad omen, whatever his Catholic mother might have said.

They picked up the key at the front desk and made their way to the elevators, careful to seem casual in case any of Raneiro's men were watching. Kane had set it up so they wouldn't have to be seen together, but Nico wasn't taking anything for granted. He'd had to leave his weapon in Monte Carlo because of airline security, but Kane had promise him another. It was a good thing; Nico felt too vulnerable without it, unable to protect Angel.

They rode the elevator to the fourth floor and made their way to room 4021, then used the key to open the door. The room was dark and quiet until they closed the door behind them. Then Kane stepped out of the shadows and turned on the light, and Nico saw that there were three additional people in the room.

Nico confirmed that the room had been swept for cameras and listening devices, and they went over the plans for that night one more time. Kane's men would be in place well in advance, hiding in one of the shipping containers on the dock that was to be their meeting place. No one had been alerted to their presence — not even the dock managers and shipping directors. Rome belonged to Raneiro. No one here could be trusted.

Nico and Angel would both carry weapons, even though they were sure to be frisked. It's what they would have done if the FBI hadn't been watching, and it was important that they behaved exactly as they would have otherwise, right up until the moment when Raneiro was taken into custody.

Wiring them wasn't an option — it would be discovered in a thorough frisk — but the surrounding area would be wired ahead of time, and Kane and his men would be watching and listening.

They went over the plan three times, covering their bases, making small changes where it seemed necessary until there was nothing else to discuss. Then everyone else left them alone with Kane.

"How are you feeling?" Kane asked when everyone was gone.

"Good," Nico said. "Ready to get this over with."

"How about you?" he asked, touching Angel's shoulder.

"Fine," she said.

Nico knew she was lying. She'd been quiet all day and had only eaten a few bites of toast at breakfast. He'd asked her about it, encouraged her to eat, but she'd said she was nervous. He couldn't blame her, but seeing her so unsettled made him want to kill Raneiro all over again. It was his fault they were in this position. His fault they hadn't already left this all behind.

"Good," Kane said. "Remember, we'll be there even though you won't be able to see us. If something goes wrong, we'll be to you in under a minute."

"Nothing better go wrong," Nico said. He was counting on Kane to help him keep Angel safe. If he thought they could do it alone, he would have.

"Everything will be okay," Kane said. "We've done this kind of thing more times than I can count. Just take the rental car to the dock. Behave exactly as you would if we weren't there, even if it seems risky. Tipping him off will be riskier, and whatever happens, we're going to get you guys out."

Nico nodded, and Kane patted his back.

"You're doing a good thing. Already the information on the Darknet file has helped us connect some dots. A lot of bad guys will be going down because of it."

Nico wanted to be glad, but right now, he only cared about bringing one bad guy to justice. Bringing one bad guy to justice and getting the woman he loved to safety.

## 47

Angel rolled down the window, breathing in the cool night air in an attempt to calm her stomach. She'd been slightly nauseous all day, and she wondered if it was the beginning of the infamous morning sickness she'd heard so much about. She hadn't been able to keep down much more than toast all day. She was hungry, but the thought of food turned her stomach. Nico assumed she was nervous.

It was a convenient enough excuse for now, but the truth was, she was less nervous than she should have been. A strange kind of calm had settled over her during the day. This was it. The final leg of their journey. They were almost there, and if everything went according to plan, she and Nico would be meeting up with David in days. She would be able to tell Nico about the baby. They would be able to start again.

She tried not to think about something going wrong. They'd come this far. They had justice on their side, not to mention Kane and the FBI. She was trying to put aside her newly learned skepticism. Trying to relearn how to hope again. Only time would tell if it was something she could regain.

They made their way through the city, the old streets as beautiful as she remembered, lights casting a soft yellow glow on the pavement. She saw the Colosseum lit up in the distance and remembered the night Nico had taken her there, kissing her in the shadow of all that history when they were just beginning to create their own. They'd come such a very long way together, and she looked over at him, taking in the straight line of his back, the look of concentration on his strong face as he navigated down to the waterfront.

He glanced over at her. "What are you smiling about?"

"Was I?" she asked.

He nodded.

"I just love you, that's all," she said.

He reached over and grabbed her hand. "That's all I need," he said.

They reached the loading area for the cargo ships that plied the waters off the coast, and Nico made his way through a series of turns. He'd been here before. They reached a sign that read 728, and he pulled into the shadows and cut the lights on the car.

"Say the word and we'll leave," he said to her.

She shook her head. "We're too close. Let's finish it."

He leaned over, kissed her hard. "You're the bravest woman I know."

Nico had said a lot of wonderful things to her. Had told her she was beautiful, professed his love countless times. But now a lump formed in her throat. She'd never known someone as good and brave as Nico Vitale. That he might think her either of those things moved her in ways she couldn't explain.

"You ready?" she asked.

He nodded.

"Have the file?"

He held up a flash drive. "Let's do it."

They made their way farther into the shadows of a massive metal hangar, their footsteps echoing across the cavernous space. The area was strangely deserted, and Angel wondered if Raneiro had paid off people to make themselves scarce while he did business. She felt exposed, visible from all angles while she couldn't see a thing beyond the column of light cast from the dock outside the hangar. Undoubtedly Raneiro was out there right now, fucking with them, letting them feel like the sitting ducks they were until he was ready to reveal himself.

As if on cue, she heard his voice from the darkness in front of them.

"Stop right there please."

They did, and he emerged into the small beam of light flanked by two men dressed in black. Angel registered their presence but not much else. She was too focused on Raneiro, the architect of her pain. All of her hatred came back in a rush. She itched to reach for the gun in her jeans. Itched to pull the trigger and rid the world of him once and for all, whatever the consequences to herself. She remembered the baby and forced herself to take a deep breath.

One step at a time.

"We have the file," Nico said. "Just like you asked."

"I'm afraid we're going to have do a little weapons search," Raneiro said. "We live in a dangerous time."

Nico held out his arms as the two men came toward them. One of them patted him down while the other one worked on Angel, running his hands up her thighs, lingering over her breasts and her crotch.

"Better tell your man to hurry with the girl before I break his arms," Nico said.

Raneiro chuckled as the men relieved Nico and Angel of their weapons. Then Angel was standing in front of Raneiro Donati with nothing at all that could kill him.

"I have to admit that I'm impressed," Raneiro said. "I wasn't sure you could do it."

"Oh, ye of so little faith," Nico said.

"It wasn't an easy task," Raneiro said.

"But not impossible for someone with your resources. Why didn't you have one of your men do it before now?"

He was getting Raneiro talking. Keeping him conversational in the hopes that he'd get Raneiro to admit he knew what was on the file. The admission would be critical to the FBIs case. Otherwise, Raneiro could claim he thought it was something else, and then he might go free.

"As you've surely come to realize, Sean Murdock isn't someone to be trifled with. I couldn't afford to incite his ire against the Syndicate, especially with his technical knowledge."

He had sold Nico down the river to Sean Murdock, knowing that even if Nico got away from the Syndicate, he'd be still be on the run from Sean Murdock for the rest of his life. The knowledge reignited her anger. Had the timing of any of it been coincidence? Or had Raneiro orchestrated everything to see that Nico would be alienated from the Syndicate, knowing that he was the one person who would go after the Darknet file to buy his freedom with the woman he loved?

"But send an estranged member," she said, "someone you've already disavowed, and you can claim ignorance."

He clapped his hands, and the sound echoed off the metal walls surrounding them. "Smart and pretty. You've done well for yourself, Nico, in spite of her pedigree."

The reference to her father was below the belt, and Nico put an arm out in front of her as if to stop her from doing something rash.

Raneiro held out his hand. "Let's see it," he said. "It's theft has caused quite an upheaval in certain circles."

Nico removed the flash drive from his pocket. "There's some really nasty stuff on here, Nero. I have to admit that I'm disappointed."

Angel recognized Nico's old pet name for Raneiro. Would it inspire him to keep talking?

"You've always romanticized our business, Nico. Always refused to see it for what it is. If you'd been more honest with yourself about it, you might have inspired fear in your men instead of disdain."

"You're right," Nico said. "I believed things could change. That was my biggest mistake. But there's a big difference between drug running and weapons trafficking. Why go after the Darknet file? Why seek out information that will allow you to step into black market weapons sales — something that has no honor code, no tradition?"

"Violence is its own tradition," Raneiro said. "It will never cease to be part of our world, whatever the pacifists try to tell you. The only thing to do is to step aside and become a casualty or use it to make you stronger. To make sure you are one of the few who remain standing when law and order meets its inevitable demise. You've chosen to step aside. I've chosen to become stronger — and richer."

"By stealing information on weapons that are responsible for the killing of innocent people all over the world?" Nico asked him. "Weapons that bring about the demise you're talking about?"

Angel held her breath. This was it. An acknowledgement by Raneiro that he'd specifically sought out the information Nico was referring to would be enough for the FBI to make the case that Raneiro had intended to broker illegal weapons — and that would be enough to put him away for a long time.

He smiled. "You're either a victim of change or an agent of it, Nico. The Darknet file will allow me to be an agent, and that is an infinitely more powerful position."

Angel barely had time to register that Raneiro had said the words before chaos erupted around her.

She saw Raneiro's men raise their weapons first, aiming at something over her shoulder. Gunfire broke out a moment later, and she felt the jolt of concrete as her body was slammed to the ground.

Nico was covering her body with his as Kane's men moved in clad head to toe in black tactical gear.

"FBI! Lower your weapons!" Kane shouted.

But Raneiro's men weren't the kind of men to surrender. They open fired instead, spraying the surrounding area with bullets. Angel covered her head, adrenaline coursing through her body. Her mind was a jumble of observations as gunfire was exchanged.

Nico was exposed. Risking his life to save hers.

She was carrying their baby.

No one here was going down without a fight.

Where was Raneiro?

She dared a glance up and saw that one of his men was down, blood seeping from a wound in his head. The other one was on the ground, too, dragging himself backward toward the safety of one of the crates lining the walls. He was hit in the leg, maybe more than once.

But Raneiro was still there, seemingly unmoved by the ten FBI agents moving toward him.

"Lower your weapon," Kane shouted. "This place is surrounded. You're not getting out of here alive unless it's in handcuffs."

Silence seemed to thin the air in the hangar as Raneiro studied Kane. Angel thought he should be scared, or at least concerned about the situation in which he found himself. But his expression was placid; the expression of someone resigned to whatever the fates had in store.

She didn't know who fired first. There was an explosion in the room, the sound echoing off the metal walls, making her ears ring until she couldn't hear anything but a high pitched whine. Raneiro was on the ground now, but not dead: sliding toward the wooden crates, his hands empty.

And there was something else.

His gun had landed just a couple of feet from where she and Nico lay on the ground. She could reach it. If she hurried, she could reach it. Then she could kill him. End this once and for all. Never have to worry about him again.

"Put your hands over your head," Kane said. "Nice and slow."

There was a brief moment of indecision. She saw it on Raneiro's face, a reflection of her own as she eyed the gun only inches from her fingertips. Then he reached behind his back and Kane's men opened fire. The force sent Raneiro sprawling.

There was a split second of shocked silence in the moment before Kane's men moved toward the dead bodies. And then Nico was sitting up, holding her head between his hands, scanning her frantically for signs of injury.

"Are you okay?" he asked. "Are you hurt?"

She saw Raneiro's gun, still on the ground, over Nico's shoulder, as she felt the spread of wetness between her legs. She looked down to see a circle of blood seeping across the crotch of her jeans. Nico's eyes followed hers, confusion shadowing his features.

He pulled her into his arms. "Help! We need help over here!"

# 48

ONE YEAR LATER

The sand was soft under her sandals as Angel stopped at one of the market stands to admire a swath of green silk.

"Ini adalah indah." Angel spoke in Balinese to the elderly woman manning the kiosk.

"Terima kasih. Itu di desa saya," the woman replied.

"Harganya berapa?" Angel asked, running the soft fabric between her fingers.

"Dua puluh tujuh tiga puluh tiga rupiah." The woman's face was grave as she quoted the price. Negotiating in Bali was serious business.

Angel nodded, handing over the appropriate bills.

Their agreement reached, the woman's face broke into a wide smile. "Keputusan yang baik."

*A good decision.*

Angel returned her smile and scanned the beach in the distance. Tourists mixed with locals, spread out on the sand and playing in the water, their bathing suits and umbrellas and towels dotting the landscape like the prayer flags strung throughout Bali's landscape. A gentle breeze drifted in off the water, caressing the skin of her shoulders, bare under her tank top, lifting the edges of her long skirt and the loose tendrils of her hair.

A good decision indeed.

She placed the bundle of fabric inside her bag and gave the woman one more smile before turning her attention back to the market. She walked slowly, in no particular hurry. She would go back to the cottage soon, cut up some of the fresh fruit she'd bought for lunch. Later, she and Nico would go to the orphanage where David volunteered his time. Maybe he would finally tell Angel about his love for the soft-eyed Balinese boy who worked there with him.

She was almost to the end of the market when she caught sight of a man moving toward her. He wore linen pants and a loose shirt, the easy flow of the clothes only providing a hint of the strength and muscle that lay under the fabric.

And in his heart.

*Nico...*

He was a warrior. He'd saved her life. Maybe even her soul.

His eyes were shaded with sunglasses, but she knew the instant he saw her, saw it in the lift of his mouth, the smile that was meant only for her. He moved more quickly, anxious to get to her, and she felt the tug of her body to his. But now there was something else.

The tug of her spirit to his, her heart.

They belonged together. They always had.

She met him halfway, then reached down to touch the bundle cradled in the fabric against his chest.

Their daughter.

Angel touched the soft fuzz of the baby's head, lowered her lips and inhaled her familiar, sweet scent. She was all the more precious for the fear Angel had felt in Rome when she thought she might have lost her. They had rushed Angel to the hospital, run a little instrument over her belly until they'd heard the soft locomotive of the baby's heartbeat.

*Choo… choo… choo…*

Nico had lowered his head to her belly and cried.

She'd been put on bed rest as a precaution, and she and Nico had holed up in London until the danger to the baby had passed. David had joined them a short time later, and they'd even had a brief visit from Luca, who had announced that he always wanted to be an uncle. He was on his way to Miami, and she'd hugged him tight, fighting tears as she said goodbye. She had a feeling they'd see him again someday.

Braden Kane had kept them posted about the trial that had prosecuted Sean Murdock for espionage, illegal trafficking, and a host of other crimes that would keep him in prison for the rest of his life. But the world was used to his software, and his business legacy would survive him. It didn't seem fair, but it was something Angel could live with. Raneiro Donati was dead, and while she liked to think she wouldn't have gone for the gun, wouldn't have pulled the trigger herself, she would never really know.

She and Nico and David had settled in Bali before the baby was born. Angel and Nico had been married in a small ceremony on the beach, and Angel had given birth in their cottage by the sea, aided by one of the local midwives and Nico, who had looked at her with such love when he first held their daughter that Angel had wept.

"Hello, beautiful," Nico said, touching her hair.

She smiled up at him. "Hello. How is she today?"

"An angel," he said. "Just like her mother."

She stood on tiptoe, kissed his lips. "Ready for lunch?"

"I'm ready for you," he said, his voice low and deep.

She grinned. "Work first, play later."

He nodded, a slow smile spreading to his lips. "Work first, play later." He touched his lips to their daughter's head. "I guess that means lunch for all of us, princess."

She took his hand, and they turned toward the water and their new beginning.

Toward life. And each other.

Reviews are such a big help to authors and readers! Please let others know how you enjoyed this book by leaving a review.

**WANT MORE FARRELL BLACK?** Order SAVAGE, the first book in the full length London Mob series.

*If I was Superman, Jenna was my Kryptonite.*

Farrell Black is dirty, dangerous, and holds nothing sacred. Growing up on the mean streets of London, he clawed his way to the top of a criminal empire with nothing but sheer force of will and the determination to need no one.

Ever.

Then he met Jenna Carver, and all bets were off — until the day she walked out of his life without a backward glance.

**Leaving him was the hardest thing she'd ever done.**

As a kid, Jenna knew how people looked at her. Like she was stupid. Worthless. Poor. So she spent her life working to become someone else. Then she met Farrell Black, and their all-consuming passion blew a hole in everything she thought she knew about herself.

**Until she was forced to make a terrible choice.**

Now Jenna is back in London for her father's funeral, desperate to avoid the one man who can banish her hard-earned reason in favor of red-hot ecstasy. But when her father's death is tied to an abuse of power at the highest levels, she has no choice but to ask Farrell for help.

As they work together to find answers to a puzzle that could have dangerous implications, desire threatens to undo them both — **and forces Jenna to choose between keeping the secret of a lifetime and having the one man who can command her body and soul.**

**WANT MORE LUCA?** Read part one of The Muscle now.

*After the turf war that almost got Luca Cassano killed, a job in Miami working as a bodyguard sounds like just what the doctor ordered; sun, sand, and a completely straightforward job.*

*But as soon as he lays eyes on Isabel, he knows that being the hired muscle will be more a lot more complicated than he imagined.*

*Isabel Fuentes knows people think she's spoiled and callous. Being the daughter of a notorious drug lord will do that to a girl, and things have only gotten worse since her father's death. Now his drug empire is run by her brother, Diego, and while their father might have been a man without a conscious, Diego is a more dangerous animal entirely.*

*At first, Isabel thinks Luca is just another hired gun. Someone to keep her from pulling the wild stunts that remind her she's still alive — that there's still hope for something else. But it doesn't take long to realize there's more than meets the eye under Luca's very hot facade.*

*And that is a complication Isabel doesn't need.*

*But when Diego reveals a nefarious reason for keeping Isabel close, she's forced to rely on Luca instead of keeping her distance. Now he may be the only one who can save her — and the one man who can bring her alive with his touch.*

**KEEP READING FOR A SNEAK PEEK**

**Please find me online. I'd love to get to know you!**

Website

Facebook
Twitter
Instagram

# The Muscle: Part One

Lucas Cassano took a swig of his beer, watching with interest as a balding middle-aged man tried desperately for the affection of a much younger woman at the outdoor bar. The man sat too close to her, his gleaming pate shining with sweat as he laughed too loud and touched her knee one too many times. The woman was obviously not impressed, and Luca watched as she leaned away each time the man got closer, her body language shouting at him to leave her alone.

Luca wanted to tell the man to back off -- both as a Public Service Announcement to him and as a favor to the woman — but he held himself in check. After months working to bring down the Syndicate and Raneiro Donati, he was in need of some much needed downtime. He loved Nico Vitale like a brother — and had grown to love Angel, the love of Nico's life, just as much — but the running and traveling and watching his back had taken its toll. Luca thought he'd been under the radar as Nico's second-in-command, but it hadn't turned out that way, and Luca had found himself out of a job and signing amnesty papers with the Feds after Raneiro was killed in Rome.

He was looking forward to his new job as a bodyguard for the progeny of one of Miami's most affluent families. That the child in question was the daughter of a well known drug kingpin didn't bother him in the least. He was done taking a personal interest in the goings-on of his employer. Now he would be nothing but hired muscle, and he was totally fine with that.

He took another drink of the beer and turned to survey the hotel property. Situated on the beach in Miami, the hotel was small compared to the monstrosities that surrounded it. He didn't mind. It felt more personal, and he admired the pool gleaming blue under the roof of the building, the sound of the ocean rushing the sand in the darkness beyond the bar.

He finished the beer and set down the empty bottle, giving the woman and older man a cursory glance as he walked past them. He wished them well, though he doubted either of them would get that they wanted tonight.

He headed toward the hotel, the property immaculately landscaped with palm trees and white lights, the pool glowing in the distance. It was early to be calling it a night, but he had to report to the Fuentes estate first thing in the morning, and he wanted to be refreshed and ready to go. The job would be an easy one, but it was always draining to start over.

He knew that better than anyone.

He'd thought his years of starting over were behind him, but he didn't bemoan the change of plan. Shit happened. You adapted and survived or you didn't survive at all. And Luca always survived. He survived as a kid, dodging his father's drunken fists, and again as an adolescent on the streets, trying to avoid social services after his father was put in jail. It hadn't been easy, but Luca had adapted quickly, learning how to protect himself with both his brain and his brawn.

Joining the Vitale family had been a turning point. There he'd found brotherhood, family. The fact that they were the East Coast arm of the Syndicate, the organization that controlled crime across the globe, hadn't mattered. Luca had done his share of illegal things in the name of survival, and the Vitale family was more conscionable than most. Nico had been like a brother to him, and Luca had pledged his loyalty without question, even when it meant making an enemy of Raneiro Donati after Nico fell in love with Angel Rossi.

Now Raneiro was dead and the Syndicate was in chaos. Those who had received amnesty were scattered to the wind, looking over their shoulders, hoping no one came after them. Everyone else was in jail awaiting trial. Nico and Angel were on a beach somewhere, finally getting the happy ending they deserved with their infant daughter. Luca was happy for them, but he wanted no part of love — especially after he'd seen what that kind of vulnerability did to a man. He was good at being alone, and while he'd had his share of affairs over the years, they'd always been brief, eventually ending because he couldn't — wouldn't — "open up".

Luca had no hard feelings. They'd been good women to the last. They deserved to be with someone who loved them, heart and soul, and Luca wasn't sure he and enough of either to go around.

He continued toward the glow of the pool. He would need to find a place to rent if he was going to stay in Miami, preferably someplace close to the beach. The ocean was the same one he saw every day in New York, but it felt entirely different. Here the water was as blue as azure, as warm as a kiss. The breeze was balmy, even a little heavy, and there was something comforting in the way it blew across his face off the water. He didn't know how long he'd stay, but right now, it felt like just what he needed.

He had almost reached the pool on his way to the lobby when something caught his eye above him. Glancing up, he had to blink to make sure he was seeing what he thought he was seeing. But yes, it was a woman, standing on the edge of the roof over the pool.

And it looked like she was about to jump.

# 2

Isabel had been about to take a running jump when the man appeared in her line of vision. He'd stepped out of the shadow like a ghost, emerging from the backdrop of music and conversation emanating from the bar on the hotel grounds.

Damn.

She froze when his he came to a stop, his head tilted upward. He'd seen her, and now she only had two choices; disappear before he could come after her or do what she came to do.

And she was no quitter.

She inched toward the edge of the roof. It wasn't the craziest thing she had done. There was the time she'd taken Diego's Audi and tested it at 160 MPH on the highway despite the fact that three cop cars were right behind her, lights on and sirens blaring. And the time she'd danced at a strip club just for the fun of it. It had only been one night, and she'd done it for free, but Diego had called her a slut for weeks afterward, threatening to send her to Columbia where she'd see what it really meant to be a whore.

She knew Diego thought she was crazy. And maybe she was. Maybe losing their father had done that to her. She'd been happy when he'd been alive. At least she thought she'd been.

Now everything was different. Diego was running the family business, and while it had never been exactly legal, it had taken a decidedly darker turn since he took over. At first Isabel tried to ignore it, burying herself in her art and avoiding the subject of the business with her brother. But then he'd started using the drugs her father made millions selling. The house in Coral Gables was increasingly patrolled by the violent, cold-eyed men who did her brother's dirty work and the drugged out women who kept him company. Days turned into weeks, which turned too quickly into months as she tried to shield Sofia from the worst of it. Pretty soon it got harder and harder to feel like she was alive. Harder and harder to feel like there was a point to it all. A future for her beyond the gilded walls of the house that hadn't felt like a home in longer than she remembered.

From the outside, it must have looked like she had options; college, travel, even getting a job just to keep busy. She had plenty of money.

But Sofia needed to be in school, needed routine and stability, and Diego always had an excuse to keep Isabel close. His reasoning sounded rational enough when he explained it to her. There was only one problem; It was all a lie.

"Hey!" the man called up from below. "What are you doing?"

His voice forced her back to the present. She froze, trying to decide what to do. The pool was just below her, the warm breeze coming off the water a caress through the flimsy fabric of her nightgown. She wasn't scared. The pool was right there. The water would welcome her with open arms. It wouldn't be so bad. And at least she would feel alive, if only for a few minutes.

She continued to the edge of the roof.

# 3

He squinted, trying to get a better look at her, but all he got were impressions — a young woman, dark hair billowing around her, a white slip or nightgown plastering itself to her skin in the breeze that rose up off the water.

He stopped in his tracks as she inched closer to the edge of the roof. What was she doing up there? Trying to kill herself?

He tried to gauge the distance from the roof to the pool. The hotel was only six stories high, and the roof above the pool was over an interior courtyard that dipped even lower than the rest of the building. He guessed it was one, maybe two stories.

Could she survive a fall from that distance if she landed in the pool?

She froze, and even from a distance he could feel her eyes connect with his, like some kind of beacon that transcended the shadows between them. She seemed to hesitate in the moment before she inched closer to the edge.

"Stop!" he shouted. "You're going to hurt yourself!"

It was a stupid thing to say -- especially if that's what she intended to do — but the words were out of his mouth before he could analyze them. His mind paged through his options, but it didn't take long to realize there weren't very many. He could make a run for the roof or stay here and try to talk her down.

Running for the roof didn't seem very smart. He'd have to take the elevator or the stairs, during which time she'd be completely out of his line of sight. She could hit the pool — or the ground — before he ever got to her. On the other hand, standing here and yelling up at the roof didn't seem very productive either. He wasn't even sure she could hear him.

He held out his hands and raised his voice. "Just wait there! I'll come up."

He eased toward the hotel, his eyes still on the girl. The clouds parted to reveal a sliver of moonlight, and he caught a glimpse of her face. It wasn't what he expected. Not tortured or sad. Just serene. Like she knew exactly what she was doing and was there to get it done. The certainty on her face scared him more than anything, and he started moving faster toward the hotel.

He was almost to the doors, almost to the point where she would disappear from view as he entered the lobby, when she reached the very edge of the roof. Dread hit his gut like a stone, and he wasn't even surprised when she leapt off the building a couple of seconds later.

He watched helplessly as she fell through the air, way too graceful for what she was doing, the white fabric billowing around her body. He wasn't aware of making the decision to run for the pool, but he reached it just as she splashed into the deep end.

He dove in without a second thought, registering with surprise that the water was warm, like everything else about Miami. He opened his eyes, trying to orient himself to the blurry underwater landscape. A moment later, she came into view, her body floating across the deep end, drifting through the water, tinged blue-green from the lights.

He swam toward her, thinking she might already be dead. But then she opened her eyes, her gaze connecting with his before she started swimming for the edge.

She was alive.

He barely had time to register the fact before anger surged through his body. What the hell had she been doing? What had she been thinking?

He swam hurriedly toward her, slowed down by the weight of his clothes, but by the time he reached her, she was already lifting herself out of the pool. Water dripped from her body, the white nightgown sticking to her skin, revealing a body he could have explored all night if only he hadn't been so pissed.

"What the fuck were you...?" he started.

She started running.

He hoisted himself out of the pool, surprised at how heavy his soaked jeans felt around his thighs, and took off after her, chasing her toward the beach, shadowed now that the moon had disappeared behind another cloud. He didn't know what he would do once he caught her, but she'd been stupid and irresponsible. At the very least he would give her a piece of his mind.

# 4

Isabel didn't expect the man to chase her onto the beach. She was alive — that was obvious — what more did he want from her?

She hurried toward the pounding surf, hoping to lose him, when a bank of clouds rolled in front of the half moon. The beach was nearly deserted, a lone couple strolling hand in hand her only company. She ran past them without making eye contact, her nightgown wet and stuck to her skin. She didn't have time to stop and explain to the man who had watched her jump from the roof of the hotel. She needed to get back to the house before Diego realized she was missing.

She ran as fast as her legs would carry her, although in hindsight, it might have been smart to spend less time painting and more time working out if she was going to try and get away from hot, muscular men on the beach.

And he had been hot. That much she'd been able to see even from the roof of the hotel.

She pushed the thought away and headed farther down the beach. There was no shelter, nothing to hide behind, but maybe if she got far enough ahead she could make it back up to the row of hotels before he caught up to her. She would be able to get lost in the crowd then, would be able to disappear. She was scoping out the light beyond the beach when she felt a hand close around her arm.

"Stop."

The voice was deep and commanding and utterly male, and when he spun her around, she went down in a flurry of sand and curse words.

"Stop it!" he said again, pinning her under his body.

She went still, her whole body suddenly primed by the hard length of him against her. They were both breathing fast, her chest rising and falling against his while he looked at her with the most piercing blue eyes she'd ever seen. They left her speechless and for a moment it was all she could do not to lift her head from the sand and press her lips to his, slip her tongue inside the full lips that were only inches from her own.

"Are you crazy?" he finally said. "What the hell was that?"

"None of your business!" She tried to shove him off her, but his body was as hard and immovable as a slab of perfectly sculpted stone. "Get off me!"

"Not until you tell me what you were doing on the roof." A lock of dark hair fell across his forehead, and she had to resist the urge to brush it back with her fingers.

"Why do you care?"

"I don't," he said. But she thought she saw a flicker in his eyes that hinted at a lie. "But I don't want to read about you offing yourself in the morning paper and know I could have done something to stop it."

She laughed, barely able to squeeze it out under the weight of his body. "I'm not suicidal."

"Then what the fuck were you doing up there?"

"I just... something I do sometimes," she said. "That's all. Now get off me!"

He still didn't budge, and she tried to ignore the lick of desire that ran through her body at the feel of his thigh pressed between her legs, his massive chest and powerful arms like the wings of a giant angel covering her. She didn't know this guy at all. He could be anybody. He could do anything to her here in the dark and no one would know the difference. She'd never see Sofia again. What would happen to her little sister then?

But despite the list of possibilities running through her mind, she wasn't afraid. There was something inherently calming about the man on top of her, something sure and protective in his blue-eyed gaze.

He finally stood. She missed the heat of him almost immediately, and she got to her feet, brushing sand off her wet nightgown, hoping he couldn't see how he'd affected her.

"What do you mean?" he asked. "Why is it something you do?"

She shook her head. "You wouldn't understand."

He crossed his big arms over his chest. "Try me."

She mimicked his action, covering her wet body with her folded arms. "No."

"No?"

"That's right," she said. "No."

His gaze pierced hers thorough the darkness and she was suddenly scared. Not of him. Of herself and all the things she didn't usually allow herself to feel.

All the things she might feel if only she wasn't so afraid.

# 5

He stared at her through the darkness, then had to force a bland expression when the moonlight streamed through a bank of clouds. She was beautiful — more beautiful even than he'd thought when he first saw her, illuminated by the lights of the city on the top of the hotel roof.

Now he could see that her skin was creamy, the color of a perfect cappuccino, as smooth and clear as fine porcelain. Her eyes had seemed brown at first, but now he saw that it was too simple a word for the complex swirl of amber and green that ran through them. Hazel? That couldn't be right. It was too pedestrian for what he saw when he looked into her eyes. There was something stubborn and wild there, something that told him she wouldn't be tamed. By him. By anyone. Something that told him there were people who had tried and failed.

But if her face was a work of art drawn by a master, her body could have been sculpted by the hand of da Vinci himself. It was lush, with full hips and a narrow waist that rose to the soft swell of her breasts. He wanted to pull down her nightgown and flick his tongue over her nipples, probably cold and wet from the pool. It was a body he could lose himself in if he could escape her eyes long enough to try, and his cock pressed painfully against the restraint of his jeans, a side effect of having her pinned beneath him in the sand.

"I was trying to help, you know," he finally said, trying to distract himself.

"I don't need your help," she said.

"That remains to be seen," he said.

"It doesn't," she said. "You don't know anything about me, but I can assure you that I'm just fine."

He caught a hint of false bravado in her voice that told him she was lying. That maybe she was a lot further from fine than she was willing to admit.

"Maybe," he said, "but you were flinging yourself from the top of a building. What did you expect me to do?"

"I didn't expect anything," she said. "I didn't think anyone would be watching."

"Well, it was a damn stupid thing to do," he said. "You could have been killed."

"But I wasn't," she said.

"You could have missed the water."

"But I didn't."

He ran a hand through his hair, already drying from his unexpected dip in the hotel pool. "Are you always this stubborn?"

"Are you always this nosy?"

"Helpful, you mean?" he asked.

She sputtered, something between a laugh and a sigh of resignation. "I have to go."     She turned away, and he felt a sudden sense of loss. He would probably never see her again. Why did he hate the thought of it?

"What's your name?" he asked.

"It doesn't matter," she said, turning away. "Thanks for the rescue."

The words were said drily, thick with sarcasm. She raised a hand in a silent farewell, and he watched the sway of her hips as she disappeared into the shadows.

# 6

Isabel made her back to the road and started walking. She could have taken a cab and paid when she got home, but she didn't want to announce the fact that she'd been out of the house in the middle of the night. Diego was already frustrated with her, already impatient with her antics. She couldn't afford to keep pissing him off. Sofia couldn't afford for Isabel to keep pissing him off.

Besides, her jump from the hotel roof hadn't been for him. It hadn't been a show of rebellion designed to get his attention or a way to make a point. In fact, she would have been totally fine if she never got his attention again.

Diego's attention wasn't usually a good thing.

No, she'd jumped into the pool for the same reason she'd done all the crazy things she'd tried in the past — to feel alive. To remind herself there was more than the mansions in Coral Gables, the prostitutes and brutish criminals Diego kept like pets in the house that had belonged to their father. Their family.

It took her almost an hour to reach the gated property, but she didn't mind. She used the time to let her mind wander, to think about the new piece she was working on, about Sofia and how to make things normal and safe for her. When she finally got home, she made her way to the back fence and the hole in the elaborate security system set up by her father before his death. It had taken her awhile to find the gap in the camera coverage, and she was half-surprised it hadn't been discovered by Diego after one of her many exploits. She'd heard him rail to the men who were tasked with securing the property, heard him demand they find out how she was getting out of the house. But none of them were very bright, and they'd never nailed down her ability to sneak in and out of the house unnoticed.

The last time she'd been caught was when the police brought her home after her joy ride in Diego's car. If she'd managed it unseen, she would have ditched the car in a good part of town and made it back to the house just like she was now, creeping around the perimeter of the property and hopping the fence in the dark spot, dodging the cameras as they made their slow rotation of the grounds, climbing in through the window left open almost year round to keep her room cool. She could only hope one of her brother's enemies wasn't smarter than the men who protected him.

Otherwise, they'd all be dead.

She slid through the open window and touched her feet to the marble floor of her bedroom. It was dark, the sheer curtains on her canopy bed rustling in the breeze from the open window. She stripped off her nightgown and walked naked to the adjoining bathroom, passing a row of canvases lining one of the walls. She turned the shower on hot and stepped inside. The water hit her cool skin, warming her immediately, and she tipped her head back into the spray, her mind turning to the man on the beach.

Who was he? And why had he bothered chasing her after he knew she was alive?

She poured soap into her palm and rubbed it along her full breasts, down the flat plane of her belly, between her legs.

He'd been tall and well built, with sizable biceps that had bulged when he'd crossed his arms and pecs that were on glorious display through his wet T-shirt. His thighs had been muscular and strong, but not huge like some of the guards who used the gym on the property. Lean and defined, but not beefy.

She slipped her soapy hands between the folds of her sex, closing her eyes at the memory of his thigh pressed between her legs, the pressure of it rubbing against the mound there. Her pussy clenched at the thought, and for a moment, she could almost imagine what it would have felt like to open her legs, let him slide into her.

A small moan escaped her lips, and her eyes shot open. She removed her hand from between her legs, turned toward the spray to rinse off. She couldn't afford to think about stuff like that. Sex, love… they were for some other time far in the future. For after she figured out a way to escape Diego with Sofia.

She finished rinsing off and got out of the shower. After she'd dried off, she threw on a pair of silk lounge pants and a tank top and crept out into the hallway. The house was quiet except for the soft thump of music coming from Diego's bedroom, and she hurriedly made her way to Sofia's room at the end of the hall. She slipped inside and closed the door behind her.

The room was dark except for a series of muted images thrown across the pale pink walls. Whales and dolphins and colorful fish danced across the room in pale green, light blue, and vibrant pink, casting shadows on Sofia's face as she slept.

Isabel smiled to herself and crossed the room, easing herself gently down on the bed next to her little sister. She was sound asleep, one arm flung across the big bed, her dark hair a shadow on the pillowcase. Isabel reached out and touched her cheek, lifting a stray piece of hair from her face and tucking it back on her pillow. She looked so peaceful, so innocent. Isabel felt a familiar surge of determination. She was all Sofia had now. Their father had adored them, but he was gone now, and Diego was too much of a wild card to know what he might do if Isabel didn't obey him. He was head of one of the biggest drug empires in the US. He did business with people who didn't think twice about committing horrific crimes, sometimes simply to send a message to anyone who might consider crossing them.

And Isabel was under no delusion that she was any different because she was Diego's blood.

She would have to be careful. Make plans and backup plans. Make sure everything was in place for her and Sofia to get away the first time. Because Isabel knew one thing for sure; there would be no second chance. If she tried to leave with Sofia and Diego found them, she would be dead. She couldn't even think about what that would mean for Sofia.

She leaned over, kissed her sister softly on the cheek, smiled as the little girl murmured in her sleep. Then she padded across the cold floor in her bare feet and slipped out of the room.

"What are you doing?"

The voice made her jump, and she turned to find Diego staring at her with dilated pupils, an unsettling grin on his face.

"Just checking on Sofia," she said.

"Why do you baby her so much?" Was it her imagination that he was slurring his words? Probably not. "She's almost a teenager."

"She's ten," Isabel said, her voice steely. The last thing she wanted was for Diego to start thinking their baby sister was old enough to be exposed to all his bullshit.

"Exactly," he said, leaning in close enough that she could smell the tequila on his breath. "Ten, not five."

Isabel sighed, trying to raise some semblance of sibling affection for the drunken man in front of her. She could hardly remember him as a child. Had he been nice? Had they loved each other? She thought they must have, but it seemed as impossible now as the moon rising in the morning instead of the sun.

"I'm just looking out for her, *hermano*. She misses Papa so much."

It had been the wrong thing to say. Diego saw any mention of their father as an unflattering comparison. His eyes darkened, and he swore in Spanish. "Papa is dead. I'm Sofia's papa now." He grinned. "And yours."

Isabel held her anger in check for Sofia's sake. "No, *carnal*. You're our brother, and we love you very much."

His face softened, and he leaned in, pulled Isabel into an almost-painful embrace. "You think you're so smart, *niña*," he murmured, grabbing a fistful of her hair hard enough to make her eyes water. "Just don't get too smart now."

Isabel forced herself to kiss his cheek. "Don't worry, *mi hermano*. All is well."

A door opened and a skinny blonde with a bad spray tan stumbled naked into the hall. "Where are you, baby?" she whined. "I woke up and you were gone."

Diego turned away from Isabel and started back toward his suite of rooms. "Just talking to my sister, the *punta*," he said.

The girl laughed, and a minute later they both disappeared behind the closed door. Isabel leaned against the wall, exhaling a breath she hadn't realized she was holding.

She had to get out of here. And soon.

# 7

Luca was up with the sun the next morning. He went for a run on the beach — his new favorite routine since moving to Miami — and returned to the hotel. He ordered room service, took a quick shower, and threw on his slacks just in time to open the door for his food.

Today he would meet his employer, Diego Fuentes. Of course, he'd done his research before his interview with Hector Diaz, Diego's head of security. But Luca knew that the information found online was usually a pale version of what was more often than not a complex story.

What he did find out is that Diego's father, Silvio, had reportedly run one of the biggest drug channels in the country before his death the year before. Rumor had it that Diego was heir to the business — and he wasn't exactly the best man for the job. According to the gossip columns online, Diego was best known for playing the part of wealthy playboy. There were plenty of pictures to back up the claims — Diego draped with women at exclusive clubs, sunning himself on his yacht, smoking a cigar surrounded by suited men in darkly lit rooms.

But there were other rumors, too. Rumors of violence and brutality that made even Luca hesitate. It's not like he was sheltered. He'd worked for the Syndicate since Nico had pulled him off the street, and while Nico had prided himself on running an efficient, modern version of the old-school mob, there had been plenty of violence.

Still, rumors of Diego's crimes had initially made Luca hesitate to accept the job. Then he'd reminded himself that it wasn't his job to pass judgement, and it definitely wasn't his job to try and figure out how much of what he'd read was true. For all he knew, every word had been fabricated by the tabloid vultures who fed on bad news and created it out of thin air when there wasn't any. Besides, Luca had followed his conscience with Nico and Angel, had helped them escape Raneiro and start over with David, Angel's brother. Luca didn't want to know everything anymore, didn't want to be part of the inner circle. He just wanted to show up for work, put in his time, and go home to the beach, a beer, and sometimes, a woman in his bed.

But he had to admit to being curious. Diego was supposedly only twenty-eight, and Luca couldn't help wondering what that kind of power and violence would do to someone so young. It softened his conscience to know that he had been hired to protect Diego's little sister. Apparently, there were two of them —one in her early twenties and one who was only ten years old. Luca didn't have a lot of experience with kids, but he liked them well enough, and protecting a kid would be nice change from watching the backs of men who had a talent for getting themselves into trouble.

A glance at his phone told him he was cutting it close. He left his tray outside the room, then slipped on the pale blue button down he'd set aside. He grabbed his jacket on the way out of the room and headed to the valet where he gave them the ticket for  Nico's red LaFerrari. Luca had felt bad taking the car, but Nico didn't need it anymore, and if Luca hadn't taken it the sleek vehicle would have been sold off to someone who might not appreciate it.

And that would have been a crying shame.

The drive to the Fuentas estate took him less than half an hour. He pulled up outside two imposing stone pillars and an iron gate, then gave his name to a voice from the intercom. A moment later, the gates swung open, and he pulled up a brick drive that wound through palm trees and led to a large white house fronted with columns. A meaty guy in a suit was standing out front, arms crossed in front of him. It was a position with which Luca was intimately familiar. It was designed to send a message.

I'm watching you. And whatever you're thinking about doing - don't.

Luca pulled the car to a stop in front of the house, stepped out, and confidently approached the man. There were protocols that went along with working in a group of dangerous men. Showing that you were willing to be part of the team was number two on the list — right after making it clear that you could hold your own.

"Luca Cassano," he said to the man.

He nodded. "Robert. Hector sent me to bring you in."

"Where should I park the car?" Luca asked.

"Leave the keys," the man said. "Someone will move it."

Luca hesitated. He wasn't crazy about someone else driving the LaFerrari, but making an issue of his hot car wasn't going to win him any points with his new coworkers. Besides, Luca had learned a long time ago that things were replaceable. Over the years he'd replaced furniture, clothes, and yes, even cars. There was something freeing about being unattached, and Luca planned to keep it that way. He handed over the keys without another word.

He followed Robert into the house, making a point not to stare too openly at the expansive foyer, the staircase that wound to the second floor behind an iron banister, the expensive marble underfoot. It's not like he hadn't been in a nice house before. Nico had some of the most beautiful properties Luca had ever seen. But it never ceased to surprise him how many people had so much, and he could never quite reconcile himself as one of them. It didn't matter that he had millions stashed in an offshore account thanks to his work with the Vitale family. Part of him still felt like the orphaned homeless kid, sleeping in cheap motels and under overpasses, eating out of dumpsters.

"You've done this kind of work before?" Robert asked as they headed down a long tiled hallway.

"More or less. Although never assigned to one person," Luca said.

Nico didn't count. Luca had been Nico's Underboss, which made him Nico's employee, not his babysitter.

"The girl's a handful," Robert said. "Lost two guards in the last month alone."

"They quit?" Luca asked.

Robert met his gaze, and Luca realized the man's pupils were so dark they were almost black. "Something like that."

He opened the double doors to the study and indicated that Luca should go inside. Luca did, and the doors shut quietly behind him. The room was large, with elaborately carved furniture and expensive rugs. The ocean beckoned through large, multi-paned windows, and a set of double doors were left open to let in the breeze. It felt almost too lavish; the intricacy of the furniture, the gilded wood framing the art, the vibrant colors outside the windows. All of it felt overdone compared to the sleek elegance of New York.

"It's nice to see that you made it," an accented voice said to his right.

He turned to find Hector Diaz regarding him from the edge of the room. The man wasn't intimidating — Luca was rarely intimidated by anyone — but there was something unsettling about his gaze. Cold and slippery, it was the gaze of someone lying in wait. Luca didn't know what the other man was waiting for, but Luca would have to be ready in case it turned out to be him one day.

He pushed the thought away. He was here to do his job. Babysit the little girl. Go home and eat dinner. Watch the water from the windows of his yet-to-be-rented house.

"I did," he said, holding out his hand. "Nice place."

Hector shook his hand. "Have you found a place to live?"

"Still working on it," Luca said. "But I'm sure it won't take long."

"Nonsense," Hector said. "You'll stay here. There's plenty of room."

Luca hid his surprise. No one had said anything about room and board being part of the package. He valued his privacy, now more than ever, and had no desire to live under the same roof as someone like Diego Fuentes.

"That's won't be necessary," he said.

Hector clasped his shoulder, his grip steely, and Luca had to resist the desire to wrap his hands around the other man's wrists, take him down, press his face to the cold marble floor.

"It will be easier for you to do your job here," Hector said. "You must trust me on this." Luca hesitated, trying to think of a gracious way to decline the offer. Hector spoke again before he could answer. "At least until you find something more permanent, yes?"

It was a rhetorical question. Luca knew had no choice but to accept the offer if he didn't want to rouse suspicion — always a concern when working with those who made their money illegally — or create bad feelings.

He nodded. "Thank you."

"It is no problem. You can bring your things when you come tomorrow." Hector reached into his jacket and handed Luca a cell phone. "This is your duty phone. Keep it on at all times."

Luca slipped it into his pocket. "Anything else I should know?"

Something secretive dropped over Hector's eyes. "Why don't you take a tour of the house, meet your charge? We can talk afterwards."

"That works," Luca said.

Hector surveyed him for a long moment. "You know that you are employed by Diego Fuentas, yes?"

"That's my understanding," Luca said.

"Good," Hector said. "It is an important thing to remember."

Luca was still trying to decipher the hidden meaning behind the words when Hector opened the door. Robert appeared a moment later, and they made their way out into the hall.

"This is the main part of the house," Robert said, leading him through an enormous living room with high, rustically-beamed ceilings. "You'll only be here if the job requires it."

Luca listened as Robert led him through the house, down hallways that led to more hallways, all of them tiled or floored with marble, some of them covered with rugs. There was a media room and a library, something that looked like an art studio dotted with expressive, vibrantly colored abstracts, an expansive Spanish style kitchen and dining room. The grounds were just as elaborate, screened off from the other wealthily inhabitants of Coral Gables with large trees and fences. At the back of the house, an infinity pool seemed to meet the sea beyond it, and a large, covered palazzo with columns like the ones at the front of the house offered shelter to half a dozen teak lounge chairs.

When they were done with the house, Robert led the way upstairs to the second floor via a less elaborate staircase at the back of the house. "Diego prefers we use the back staircase unless it's necessary to use the front."

"Will do," Luca said as they emerged into a tile hall lined with sconces, fine art, and more of the carved furniture that he'd seen on the ground floor.

The continued down the hall to a door on the right. Robert opened it without knocking and stepped into the room.

"Hello, Sofia," he said.

Luca's eyes followed the other man's gaze to a girl reading on the bed, her long dark hair pulled into a ponytail over big brown eyes and delicate features.

"Who's that?" the little girl asked.

"This is Luca," Robert said. "He'll be staying here for awhile."

Luca was trying to figure out how best to introduce himself to the small, serious creature in front of him when she spoke again.

"Is he Isabel's new bodyguard?"

Isabel…

Luca scrolled the research he'd done on the Fuentes family and had only just started to connect the dots when a familiar woman stepped into the room.

It couldn't be…

But it was. The woman from the hotel roof, the one he'd chased down the beach. The one who had stirred his body and his imagination when he'd pressed against her on the sand.

A flicker of surprise flashed in her eyes in the moment before she returned her expression to one of boredom.

"Don't worry, *mija*," she said to Sofia. "He won't last any longer than the others."